GHOST STORIES
STORIES
of
PENNSYLVANIA

Dan Asfar

Lone Pine Publishing International

© 2002 by Lone Pine Publishing International Inc.
First printed in 2002 10 9 8 7 6 5 4 3
Printed in Canada

The Publisher: Lone Pine Publishing International
Distributed by Lone Pine Publishing
1808 B Street NW, Suite 140
Auburn, WA 98001
USA

Website: www.lonepinepublishing.com
          www.ghostbooks.net

National Library of Canada Cataloguing in Publication Data

Asfar, Dan, 1973–
  Ghost stories of Pennsylvania

  ISBN-13: 978-1-894877-08-4
  ISBN-10: 1-894877-08-X

  1. Ghosts—Pennsylvania. 2. Legends—Pennsylvania. I. Title.
GR110.P4A83 2002   398.2'0974805   C2002-910969-8

Editorial Director: Nancy Foulds
Project Editor: Chris Wrangler
Illustrations Coordinator: Carol Woo
Production Coordinator: Jennifer Fafard
Cover Design: Elliot Engley, Gerry Dotto
Layout & Production: Jeff Fedorkiw, Elliot Engley
Photo Credits: Every effort has been made to accurately credit photographers. Any errors or omissions should be directed to the publisher for changes in future editions. The photographs in this work are reproduced with the kind permission of the following sources: Library of Congress (p. 25: HABS, PA, 51–PHILA, 25–2; p. 56: USZ62–100660; p. 59: USZC4–1825; p. 65: HABS, PA, 23–RAD, 1B–1; p. 77: HABS, PA, 51–PHILA, 111–15; p. 78: HABS, PA, 51–PHILA, 111H–8; p. 81: HABS, PA, 51–PHILA, 111–57; p. 126: USZ62–80540; p. 130: HABS, PA, 51–PHILA, 354–7; p. 133: HABS, PA, 7–ALTO, 110–1); Library and Archives Division, Historical Society of Western Pennsylvania (p. 21); George School (p. 71); Jean Bonnet Tavern (p. 100); Clyde Hare (p. 141); Lycoming County Historical Society (p. 153); Edrick Thay (p. 49, 52).

PC: P6

Dedication

For Patty Wilson
and all the other paranormal
raconteurs of the state

Contents

Acknowledgments

Two things are required for ghost stories to come to the public's attention: ghosts and people who are willing to talk about them. While many of us who have had experiences with the supernatural might find ourselves struggling with the question of spirits on earth, far fewer would make it a point to get these stories out to the public at large. Everyone I have spoken to in the process of writing this book falls into the latter category. They are individuals who, for whatever reason, feel that it is important to share their supernatural tales. There are a number of reasons people might feel impelled to relate such experiences.

The first explanation that comes to mind is the obviously therapeutic nature of getting such an experience out into the open. Encountering a ghost is hardly a casual occurrence. Any meeting with such an entity is also a confrontation with issues of mortality and the afterlife. These are profound issues, to say the least, which many of us tend to avoid throughout much of our lives. Is it any wonder that many of us would rather not tackle them alone? Perhaps voicing these experiences serves to shift the weight off the shoulders of firsthand witnesses and onto those of people who discuss them.

There might be another motivation for telling these tales, which could be likened to the impulse that moves a researcher to share new discoveries. A society benefits from the attainment of new knowledge, whatever that knowledge may be. Ghost stories are rarely limited to dead spirits that terrify the living during evening hours. They almost always teach us something about where they took place, be it the details of a tragedy that occurred in a haunted house, the history of a battlefield plagued with ghosts or the dramatic demise of a region's most prominent historical figure.

And then there's the matter of entertainment. There are those among us who love the idea of regaling an audience with a spine-tingling ghost story. The fact that so many people enjoy being frightened is one of those odd perplexities in the human condition, and fear and entertainment continue to remain close companions. Along with roller coasters, freak shows and horror films, the ghost story is one of the most prominent vehicles of this peculiar form of entertainment.

I have a good number of people to acknowledge for making this collection of ghost stories possible— Pennsylvanians who have not only witnessed or been aware of supernatural phenomenon, but who also have no qualms about sharing these stories with the public.

My thanks go to Patty Wilson and Scott Crownover of the Paranormal Research Foundation for providing me with information on the U.S. Hotel, the Jean Bonnet Tavern and the Mishler Theatre. Sean Snyder's investigations of the town of Tamaqua's Elks Club were an integral part of that story, while Adele Gamble, owner of New Hope's Ghost Tours, was a great help with the ghost stories of that historic town.

I couldn't have finished this book without the invaluable assistance of some of the state's historical societies, particularly the Lycoming County Historical Society for the story of Nellie Tallman's portrait and the Chester County Historical Society for researching the supernatural folklore along the southeastern border of the state. The Butler County Historical Society helped lead me to Dr. David Dixon and his account of events at the Old Stone House outside of Slippery Rock. I would also like to thank the staff at the Greene County Museum for providing me with contacts who had been researching the supernatural across the state.

My list of acknowledgments would not be complete without mentioning those writers before me who have covered the ghosts of Pennsylvania. The numerous works of master ghost story writer Charles J. Adams III have provided me with a solid base of information for a number of stories in this volume. His books, *Ghost Stories of Pittsburgh and Allegheny County, Philadelphia Ghost Stories, Ghost Stories of Berks County* and *Berks the Bizarre,* were great guides to the subject of ghosts in Pennsylvania. Mark Nesbitt proved an authority on the supernatural phenomenon in Gettysburg. And I would once again like to thank Patty Wilson, whose books, *The Pennsylvania Ghost Guide, Volumes 1 and 2,* proved entertaining and informative.

Finally, I would like to thank the staff at Ghost House Books. Their talent, diligence and patience have improved this text immeasurably. Thanks to Chris Wangler for his editorial vigilance, Carol Woo for hunting down the photographs indispensable to the layout of the book and Nancy Foulds and Shelagh Kubish for their support and confidence. Of course, I cannot conclude these acknowledgments without mentioning my writing colleague, Edrick Thay, who always manages to find the humor in every ghost story, no matter how morbid.

Introduction

One of the most remarkable things about ghosts is their persistence in popular human expression. The Ancient Greeks shook at the idea of Hades and his host of dead in the underworld, while Shakespeare's Macbeth was haunted to the point of madness by the ghost of Banquo, who would not let the cruel conditions of his murder go unpunished. Today, ghosts continue to be a central theme in innumerable stories that flood the media, be they told in books, on film or around campfires. Best-selling author Stephen King deals with supernatural forces in every second book he writes. One of his classics, *The Shining*, was adapted for film, where audiences flocked to see Jack Nicholson as Jack Torrance thrash in maniacal fits while possessed by spirits, real or imagined, in a celluloid rendition of the mountains of Colorado.

What is behind this enduring fascination with the spirits of the dead? Is there some hidden truth buried deep in the collective subconscious that continues, generation after generation, to whisper secrets into our individual intuitions? Secrets which our rational minds would rather chose to ignore? Are we so fascinated with ghosts because we know, on some primordial level, that they actually exist?

Or is this persistence of the supernatural mythos in human storytelling merely a grandiose expression of our own self-importance? Surely, the natural fear of death and the oblivion that may follow is incentive enough for us to create fanciful fables of transparent apparitions and voices in the dark—a small attempt to find comfort in the yawning of abyss of nothingness that may, fear of all fears, await us all.

But then there's the question of all the "real" hauntings that are reported now, more than ever. Every morning across America, thousands are waking up from restless nights' sleeps, disturbed throughout the night by inexplicable whispers in the dark, footsteps in the hall and cold hands on faces, around wrists, around necks. Century-old apparitions, seen by the earliest Americans in small towns and feral forests, continue to be spotted today on the concrete streets laid over the wilderness. Many of these sightings are reported in the Keystone State.

In Lebanon County, more than one Pennsylvanian has seen and heard a terrible pack of hounds tearing through the countryside over the years. Searching madly for some unknown quarry, these unearthly dogs are believed to have been killed by their cruel master over a century ago. Visitors still see all-too-eerie reminders of the horrible sacrifice Civil War soldiers paid on the Gettysburg battlefield so many years back. Transparent visions of soldiers in ragged uniforms are seen regularly among the rocks of Devil's Den, while those who stay on the crest of Little Round Top when the sun goes down might be treated to a frightening supernatural recreation of the fighting on that fateful day. These are only two accounts of ghosts among the many that are included in this volume—a book which, incidentally, only touches the surface of the supernatural world as it exists in Pennsylvania.

Certainly there are many places where ghosts would feel at home in this old state: in the streets of Philadelphia, where so much of the urban architecture was built by

18th-century hands; in the mysterious Dutch Country, where old traditions of witchcraft seem to have left discontented spirits behind; in the western part of the state, where the sensitive can still sense the horror of old conflicts that pitted settlers against Indians; and on the banks of the Delaware, where casualties of the War of Independence rub shoulders with phantom hitchhikers looking for a ride along Highway 202.

Many of these stories, told and retold over the years, have come to define a part of what the state is. Others are recent discoveries, stumbled upon by paranormal investigators, while others still involve ghosts that haven't been around long enough to be enshrined in the supernatural canon of the state.

Prepare to be introduced to the supernatural citizenry of Pennsylvania. According to sources, they are everywhere—drifting across open fields, through old buildings, magnificent churches, historic homes, down rolling streams. Do they actually exist? Well, more than a few will swear on the graves of their mothers that they do.

1
Haunted
Houses

~

More than any other possessions people claim as their own, the homes they live in reflect their personalities. Tidy or messy, modest or extravagant, houses are not only measures of people's means and living habits. They are also the havens that individuals construct against the outside world—small islands of individuality amid the vast impersonal ocean that is the public space. Our homes are ours, containing all the objects, effects and energies that are distinct to who we are.

It is no wonder, then, that people talk of houses having "personalities." Some places seem to retain an intangible energy, stemming from a sense of what the abode used to be—from the lives of its former inhabitants. And then there are those houses that are afflicted by something more than intangible energies. Distressed by some dramatic event in the past, these buildings are brought to life by spirits either unwilling or unable to move on after they have died. Despite deeds of ownership and the wishes of living inhabitants, the ghosts that drift through these haunted houses usually don't seem to be too concerned with the effect they have on the other, corporeal dwellers in the household. And while so many of us are fascinated by stories of such possessed manors, haunted houses are still places we would prefer to hear about rather than experience. What follows is a number of reports—observed from a safe distance—of people's own experiences with ghosts in their homes.

~

Ineffable Evil in Congelier House

The address of 1129 Ridge Avenue, located roughly where Route 65 meets I-279 today, can no longer be found on a map of Pittsburgh. Blown to oblivion in a massive 1927 explosion, the two-story brick building that used to stand there housed an evil energy that has since been replaced by the ceaseless flow of traffic that now moves through the area. Yet it is testament to the magnitude of the house's dark history that it still occupies a prominent place in the Steel City's folklore. To this day, many supernatural enthusiasts consider it to have been the architectural embodiment of pure evil.

The house was built by a corrupt carpetbagger named Charles Wright Congelier, who made a fortune from Civil War reconstruction in Texas. Settling into the house in 1871 with his wife, Lyda, and their young servant, Essie, he couldn't have predicted the horrors that awaited them within the walls. That isn't to say that Charles Congelier was powerless to prevent the tragedy that would soon befall his household, but the moment his lustful eyes settled on Essie, his fate was sealed.

When Lyda caught Charles and Essie in the act, she snapped. Setting upon her husband and housekeeper with a butcher knife in one hand and a meat cleaver in the other, Lyda slaughtered the pair. For days, the Congelier home was blanketed in a foreboding air of stillness, until the rancid smell brought Pittsburgh police in to investigate the suddenly silent house.

The first officers to arrive were never able to forget what they saw that day. Charles Congelier, who had been stabbed over 30 times, lay in a rank pool of gore, the handle of a butcher knife still protruding from his chest. Essie was completely decapitated; her head was lying on the floor near her body, carefully wrapped in a baby blanket. As for the perpetrator of this horrifying double homicide, Lyda was found in the ornately furnished parlor, sitting cross-legged in the middle of the dark room, soaked in blood and babbling incoherently to herself. By all accounts, Mrs. Congelier had gone completely mad.

The house remained unoccupied for the next 20 years, during which time stories began to circulate about strange sights and sounds coming from the home. People reported hearing a woman's screams from inside the house in the dead of night. Others told of frantic wails emerging from the home, as if someone within was lost in hysterical grief.

In 1892, the house was renovated to accommodate railroad workers. It quickly became apparent that something was very wrong with the building. Many of the men were awakened in the middle of the night by high-pitched screams. Others sensed that they were being watched by some unseen, malevolent presence while they lay in bed, as if someone was smoldering with intense hatred at the edge of darkness, waiting for them to fall asleep. The nocturnal hours became a nightmare for the workers, who felt those intangible eyes fall on them from that darkness, and a number of the workers suffered from lengthy spells of insomnia. When they learned the history of the house, the strange events suddenly made frightening sense, and it wasn't long before the men refused to sleep there again. Only two years after it had been purchased by the railroad company, the house was abandoned again.

The house remained unoccupied until about 1900, when it was purchased by a Dr. Adolph C. Brunrichter. The few people in the neighborhood who met Dr. Brunrichter remember him as a rather strange, jumpy man who had difficulty holding a conversation. Seldom seen by the neighbors after he moved into the house, he was soon labeled the local eccentric and left to himself. That isn't to say that they ignored him completely. People cast suspicious glances at the brick building, whispering among themselves about the strange noises that occasionally emanated from within. In addition to the accustomed wails, people began to hear the hum of electric machinery—and intermittent loud crashes.

This situation went on for about a year, until the evening of August 12, 1901, when the family living next to the Brunrichter residence was awakened by a terrifying scream, louder than anything that had come from the house before. The neighbors rushed to their windows in time to witness an explosion. Through the fabric of Brunrichter's closed curtains, they saw a red light flash through the house, followed by a fiery roar that spilled out into the night, shattering every one of the building's windows.

The grisly discovery made by the firefighters later that night shocked the entire city. Within the blackened walls of the fire-damaged house, a woman's badly decomposed body was found lashed to a hospital gurney. Leather straps bound her wrists and ankles. Her head was missing, apparently severed from her body with a clean cut of medical precision.

The head was discovered in another scorched room, grotesquely mounted before a piece of gothic machinery straight out of Mary Shelley's *Frankenstein*. Badly burnt, the dead woman's facial features were horrifically indifferent to the numerous electrodes that connected her head to a Byzantine mechanical apparatus that loomed over it. The machine was still smoking from the explosion that had ripped through the house, and it was concluded that the blast had somehow originated from the bizarre metal contrivance.

Further investigation revealed five more dead women buried in the basement floor, whose heads had been removed with the same careful precision practiced on the first corpse. It was determined that ever since the demented doctor had moved into the house, he had become obsessed with developing a way to keep people conscious after removing their heads. Legend has it that he achieved limited success in this endeavor—the shrill screams the neighbors had heard earlier that evening were purportedly issued from the head of the woman who was tied to the gurney upstairs. But the mad doctor himself was never able to confirm such speculation, for he was never seen again after that August evening.

If the house on Ridge Avenue was considered cursed before, the unveiling of Dr. Brunrichter's activities made it worse. People drew conclusions based on the final experiences of previous residents, and it was said that an evil spirit permeated the interior, driving anyone who lived there into a homicidal dementia. It did not help that the frequency of strange occurrences in the abandoned home increased dramatically after Dr. Brunrichter disappeared.

It was the emergence of a new phenomenon, however, that temporarily propelled the empty Pittsburgh home into the national spotlight. On certain nights, individuals who happened to be looking at the house would see faint flickers of light in the windows. On other nights, however, the light show in the old Congelier home was much more dramatic. Harsh eruptions of light would blaze from the house; sometimes awed observers would look on as freakish strobe effects lit the windows. Faults in electrical lines or gas connections were dismissed as culprits, because neither ran through the 19th-century house. No one could provide a definitive explanation for what was going on inside.

The inexplicable phenomena in the house attracted the attention of none other than Thomas Edison. Hoping to witness the strange events for himself, the famous inventor visited 1129 Ridge Avenue. Whatever pyrotechnic displays he saw in the home, he must have been treated to quite a show, for he left the building intent on inventing a machine that would enable people to communicate with the dead. Based on what he had seen in the Congelier home, Edison concluded that spirits manifested themselves through electrical energy. He was convinced that he could communicate with these intelligent entities if he could design a machine that would translate a spirit's electrical currents into a medium humans could understand. Alas, Edison died before his blueprints could be made into a functioning machine.

As time passed, the flashing lights that had regularly lit up the sky on Ridge Avenue began to fade. Any explanations regarding the waning lights were just as speculative as people's theories as to why the illuminations had appeared in the first place. In any case, the Congelier House story had not quite come to an end.

The noises and lights that had been coming from the house had stopped, but it was obvious to everyone who lived in the neighborhood that something very evil still remained inside. Perhaps it was the way the house always seemed to be shrouded in a veil of shadow. Even during the middle of the day, when the sun was high and not a cloud was in the sky, Congelier House somehow looked darker than its surroundings, as if it was dusk on that one lot while a brilliant noon sun shone through the rest of Pittsburgh. At night, any person walking down Ridge Avenue would pick up the pace when passing the deathly stillness of 1129. Although no sounds emerged from behind the wrought-iron fence, people swore something breathed within the inky blackness of the abandoned house—something evil that seethed with unbridled hatred.

During this time, very few people dared approach the house, let alone move in. It remained unoccupied until the early 1920s, when it was purchased by the Equitable Gas Company. The corporation's management, in search of housing for the company's immigrant workers, had no problems ignoring the building's ugly history, given how low the asking price was. Without asking a single question about the house's dubious past, the company had the home renovated, transforming it into a boarding house for their corps of poverty-line Italian immigrants.

It soon became clear that changing the building's floor plan hardly erased its past. Many of the Italian workers had been living in the house for only a few weeks when they realized that there was much more to it than brick and mortar. Men woke up in the middle of the night to hear strange murmuring voices, as if several people were whispering among themselves in the darkness. Any boarders who called out to ask who was there only woke up bunkmates who were still asleep. The phenomenon carried on for several months, with the whispering getting louder every evening. At first, the Italian immigrants assumed that the nocturnal noises were the work of the company's American employees, who were losing their jobs to immigrants working for less money—or at least that's what they desperately wanted to believe.

Truth was, the people who heard the whispers in the night had a gut feeling that they were not hearing human voices. The cold sweat, the tingling pinpricks down their backs, the unreasonable flood of horror that washed over them as they tried to decipher what was being said—those awakened by the strange sounds knew in their hearts that an inhuman presence loomed in the dark. Months passed before the intangible evil in the house decided to show the immigrants they were dealing with something much worse than a horrible dream.

One night, the boarders were just finishing eating dinner when an agonized scream rose from the basement. Upon investigation, two of the immigrants staying in the house were discovered dead in the kitchen cellar. Both men had just been killed. One was hanging from a rafter in the cellar, his neck apparently broken by his own dangling weight. The other was brutally impaled by a wooden shelf, his twisted form lying on the blood-soaked ground with the board protruding from his chest. As horrifying as the scene was, the realization that both men were killed just moments before made the event all the more shocking.

The men standing in that cellar knew that it would have been impossible for anybody to escape after the crime. Moreover, the murderer couldn't have been anybody staying in the house, because all the other boarders had been dining when they heard the scream from the cellar. Each man who stood gawking at the macabre scene was suddenly reminded of the whispers in the night. After the crime, the Equitable Gas Company couldn't pay anybody enough to sleep in the cursed house, and the house was once again emptied of all human inhabitants.

Very little was said about the house for most of the 1920s. Like the elephant in the room that no one talks about, people in the neighborhood chose to ignore the menacing building, and, as the years passed, 1129's dark history was kept alive only through the juvenile folklore of the neighborhood children. The most common challenge issued among these kids involved a foray into the "murder house," as it came to be called, but not even the bravest had the courage to crawl through the rusted gates and venture across the overgrown lawn.

In September 1927, Congelier House again appeared in the headlines of the Pittsburgh newspapers. A drunkard claiming to be Dr. Adolph Brunrichter was arrested by city police. Imprisoned while the authorities investigated his feverish confessions, the man spent most of his time delivering lengthy rants about demonic possession,

When a natural gas tank like this one exploded, Congelier House was obliterated.

torture and murder. Yet despite his maniacal admissions, police found no solid evidence linking him to the 1901 murders. It was decided that the man was more hysterical than homicidal, and he was set free after one month of incarceration. The man was never heard from again, but Congelier House was to be in the news one more time shortly after he was released.

On November 15, 1927, an explosion rocked the city of Pittsburgh. An Equitable Gas Company storage tank, full of natural gas, had somehow detonated; the resulting blast was felt all across Allegheny County, and hundreds of homes in a 20-mile radius were damaged or destroyed. People were at a loss to explain what had caused the enormous tank to explode. However, there was quite a bit of speculation that the explosion had not originated from the tank, but from nearby Congelier House. After all, the infamous brick building was the only structure that had been completely obliterated in the blast.

Since the day of the explosion, paranormal enthusiasts have had a lot of time to speculate over the evil that had occurred in Congelier House. And although no one can say for sure why so much misery occurred there, it is widely acknowledged that, while the house stood, something unholy resided in it. Whether or not this force was responsible for the explosion is anyone's guess, but even today, 75 years after the structure was consumed by fire, Congelier House lives on as one of the major hauntings in Pennsylvania's supernatural folklore.

Powel House

The Powels were New England socialites whose roots in Pennsylvania went back to 1685, the year an orphaned Samuel Powell (the original spelling of the family name) crossed the Atlantic to make a new life in the colonies. Powell secured his fortune and the wealth of his progeny by building bridges and marrying into an affluent family. He eventually became one of Philadelphia's wealthiest property owners, accumulating a fortune that was inherited by his son, Samuel Powell Jr. The second Samuel Powell, who decided to drop the second "l" from his surname, was a competent steward of the family fortune, earning considerable funds of his own as one of the city's more successful merchants. He died a loyal British subject in 1756, leaving the Powel fortune in the hands of his nine-year-old son, whom he had also named Samuel Powel.

This Samuel was the first gifted politicker to be born into the industrious Powel clan. Given possession of his inheritance when he turned 18, Samuel spent most of his younger years traveling through Europe, picking up the fine art of rubbing shoulders as he mixed with elite of other nations. By the time he got back to Philadelphia, he possessed upper-crust gentility and was fully schooled in the ways of the world. Soon after he returned, he purchased what was to become known as Powel House on Third Street. With his new bride, Elizabeth Willing, at his side, he promptly began entertaining the cream of colonial society.

Becoming friendly with such prominent figures as George Washington, Benjamin Franklin, Samuel Adams and the Marquis de Lafayette, he soon established enough political clout to win the mayoral office of the second largest English-speaking city in the world. He would be the last mayor of the colonial city. When revolution swept through the colonies in 1776, Powel sided with the revolutionaries, earning the title of the "Patriotic Mayor." He maintained his office throughout the tumultuous years of the War of Independence, and he was Philadelphia's first mayor when the city became capital of the new republic. Adding significant political power to the Powel family's well-established finances, the distinguished Pennsylvanian rose to such heights only to die in the yellow fever epidemic of 1793.

Individuals expire and times change, but many of the objects each generation creates remain standing for posterity to study and appreciate. In the case of Powel House, however, much more was left behind than mere bricks and mortar. Over the centuries, strange things have been witnessed within the exquisite Georgian mansion on Philadelphia's Society Hill. The surreal events can be explained only by using supernatural terms such as "residual energy," "ectoplasm" and "ghosts." These terms are not fanciful fictional devices intended to titillate audiences but sincere attempts at explaining the things that are going on.

Why would ghosts haunt Powel House? Many people have offered a great number of explanations as to why ghosts choose some places to haunt and not others. Although any explanation is only just a guess, there are many things that set Powel House apart from other residences.

During the colonial era, famous and influential visitors called at Powel House in Philadelphia.

What stands out most about Powel House, besides its old age and opulence, is the grandeur of the personalities who have spent time within its walls. Samuel Powel himself was a willful man whose worldly successes were certainly impressive enough to justify a desire to stay on past his given years. But besides the Philadelphia mayor, there were many other men of influence who spent time in the 18th-century mansion—powerful statesmen whose political maneuverings could affect the fate of millions. Much can be written of the historical personages who spent time inside the walls of Powel House. And much time has been devoted to the people whom Samuel Powel entertained around his dinner table.

Ever since 1965, when historian Edward Courant Moore claimed to have seen an apparition in colonial dress moving down one of the building's halls, many other sightings of unnatural entities have been reported by numerous people. According to Moore, the figure he saw bore an unmistakable resemblance to portraits of the Marquis de Lafayette. A navy blue military frock with golden epaulets on the shoulders, white tights, a saber and a tricolor sash tied around his waist—the details of Moore's description were unmistakably reminiscent of the dark-haired French revolutionary.

Lafayette is not the only spirit who has been spotted in Powel House. Mrs. Moore, Edward's wife, is said to have encountered a beautiful young woman in a beige and lavender dress, sitting in elegant repose and fanning herself in the drawing room. According to Mrs. Moore's account, the transparent lady looked at her and smiled before slowly fading into nothingness. Although Mrs. Moore was able to give a detailed description of this woman's appearance, no one knows for certain exactly who she would have been.

Mrs. Moore was not the only person to see this ladylike apparition. One history buff was visiting Powel House during the evening when he had his own run-in with the woman in beige. He was using the bathroom on the second floor when the lights suddenly went out, leaving him in total darkness. Feeling his way out of the room, he was in the hallway when it felt as if he had just wandered into a giant freezer. The man stopped in surprise, unsure what to make of the abrupt change in climate, when a strong, stifling odor grew thick in the air around him. An instant later, he felt someone grab his hand. In the dead darkness of the house, a cold damp hand gently gripped his own and began leading him to the stairway.

In the next moments, the lights flickered back on, revealing his guide for a few brief seconds. The bewildered man was standing speechless, staring at a lady whom he would later describe as the most beautiful woman he had ever seen, adorned in a beige and lavender dress that hung from her shoulders in lush folds. She was staring straight at the man she had just guided out to the stairs. Just as a subtle smile began to form on her lips, she vanished.

Other witnesses have claimed to have seen the figures of Continental Army officers moving up the stairs of the building. The wall behind these semi-transparent apparitions was visible through them, and their footfalls made not a sound.

Although the staff at Powel House are aware of the stories circulating about the building, they do not formally acknowledge the presence of ghosts there. Nevertheless, the mansion has become a regular stopping place for at least one of Philadelphia's ghost tours, in which people curious about the supernatural are taken to some of the city's famous haunted sites. And although many visitors to Powel House are interested in the affairs of the past, a good number of the site's yearly visitors have more of an interest in the supernatural than the purely historical. It seems that whether they like it or not, the curators at Powel House will have to get used to the paranormal buzz attached to the old building. As for the ghosts there, who knows when some grand old statesman from the 18th century will be seen drifting through the halls, or when the mysterious woman in beige and lavender will appear to once again bewitch some hapless man on this side of the grave?

Aaron Burr House

Aaron Burr's lifetime accomplishments—besides graduating from Princeton at the top of his class, being appointed governor of New York and eventually winning the vice-presidency of the United States—include being charged with treason and murder. More than one supernatural tale is associated with this infamous 18th-century American statesman and his family. For example, legends surround his wife, Eliza Jumel, who is said to still haunt the oldest house in Manhattan, Morris–Jumel Mansion. Burr's daughter, Theodosia, drowned in the Atlantic when the ship she was on foundered in stormy waters. According to one eerie story, the spirit of the young woman was trapped in her disturbingly life like portrait, which washed ashore on the outer banks of North Carolina a few days after the ship sank. And then there are the stories of the spirit of Aaron Burr himself.

Apparently, Burr's spirit smashes dinnerware and moves chairs from underneath patrons in One if by Land, Two if by Sea, a romantic restaurant in New York City. But if there is any place he would call home, it must be Aaron Burr House, one of the buildings in the Wedgwood Historic Collection of Inns in New Hope, Pennsylvania.

The old Victorian house, built sometime in the 1860s, wasn't always known as Aaron Burr House. Oddly enough, the building was constructed well after Aaron Burr had passed away, and although Burr was quite familiar with the area around New Hope, no monumental historical event occurred there to justify attaching Burr's name to it. Instead, the building became the setting for a constant string of minor events, strange and unusual, that have impelled people to look into its past.

The ongoing inquiry has made Carl Glassman, one of the proprietors of the Wedgwood complex, into something of an expert on Aaron Burr. The spirit of the treacherous old statesman is believed to cause the "ghostly goings-on," as Mr. Glassman calls the otherworldly events that take place.

Underneath the impressive Aaron Burr House lies a stone foundation that is even older than the wood structure built atop it. Glassman discovered that this stone pediment dates back to colonial times, and that Aaron Burr had briefly hidden in the stone cellar during troubled times.

Burr and Alexander Hamilton had been political rivals and personal enemies for over 20 years when public rivalry and a mutual deep-seated enmity led them to resolve their differences at gunpoint. On the morning of July 11, 1804, the two men stood on a grass ledge overlooking the Hudson River. Dressed in their finest clothing, they picked their pistols, loaded them and stood back-to-back, both determined to endure the duel as honorably as they could. For centuries, the practice of dueling had claimed the lives of thousands of male gentry throughout Europe. On this morning in North America, another man was about to fall.

Some accounts have Burr firing first, shooting his opponent through the heart before the man was able to raise his pistol. Other versions tell of Alexander Hamilton turning around to face Burr with hard determination, waiting for Burr to take his shot. Perhaps he hoped that Burr would miss when he fired, become touched by Hamilton's courage and abstain from shooting or simply lose heart and call off the duel before it began. But wishful thinking stands little chance against speeding bullets, and the tragedy at Weehawken, New Jersey, reached its bloody conclusion when Burr raised his pistol, aimed and, with all the hard-hearted deliberation a lengthy rivalry could produce, shot the prominent Federalist through the heart.

Burr's political ambitions were snuffed out the moment he fatally wounded Hamilton, and he was soon fleeing from the scene of the crime with the authorities from New York and New Jersey hot on his trail. Federalist media reported the duel as an ambush, and few people were willing to lend Burr a hand in the days following the murder. With the country roused against him and no friends in sight, Aaron Burr headed for the first haven he could think of: New Hope, Pennsylvania, home to the Coryell family, lifelong friends of the Burrs. The ferry near New Hope was owned by the Coryells, and Burr was whisked across the Delaware under cover of darkness and then hidden in the building on the site of the yet-unbuilt house that would, centuries later, bear his name.

Burr hid in the building for a number of days, rarely venturing out of the basement, while his protectors worked on a way to get him as far away from the area as they could. His enemies were everywhere, and when the Coryells finally were able to arrange passage to safety, Aaron Burr was whisked away to South Carolina, where his daughter, Theodosia, waited.

Most of us can only imagine the distress Burr must have felt while he was stuck in the Coryells' basement during the days after Hamilton's death. If the idea of appearing before a court of law with a murder charge was unattractive enough, the thought of being found by a lynch mob must have been even worse. Burr's stay in the house could not have been nearly as pleasant as that of visitors today, who enjoy the amenities of the bed and breakfast that stands there today. Although Burr's emotional trauma might seem a distant memory to the guests that stay at Aaron Burr House nowadays, something of the corrupt old statesman still lives on in the building, apparently intent on reminding visitors that the building is more than a place for comfort and relaxation.

The most common supernatural phenomenon in the inn is called the "sightless stare of Aaron Burr." Visitors who fall under this ghostly gaze claim that an unexpected wave of cold washes over them and that they are struck by a strong feeling that someone is staring at them. "You can feel two eyes staring at the back of your head," Carl Glassman explains. "It's a furtive, cautious glance, as if the hiding man is uncertain whether you are a friend or foe." The feeling of being watched always occurs in the same place, at the top of the stairs leading down to the stone basement, as if someone is standing at the base of the stairs, staring up from the darkness. Many individuals have quickly turned the basement light on, certain that there was someone there, only to see an unoccupied staircase descending into the empty basement.

Carl Glassman has also taken to advising visitors that if they feel something tugging at the door when trying to leave, they should speak into the air, saying, "Mr. Burr, please, I want to go out." It seems this request is reason enough for the suspicious spirit to release his grip on the door, perhaps trusting that the person will not betray his presence to his pursuers of nearly two centuries ago.

Visitors to Aaron Burr House are also advised not to make too much of creaking sounds that might be heard in the middle of the night. "That's only the colonel," guests are told, referring to Aaron Burr's rank when he served in the Revolutionary Army. Judging by the sound of the slow, careful footsteps that have been heard creeping across the ground floor after the sun has set, it seems that during his time here Burr may have ventured out of his hiding place a few times during the night. We may never know exactly what Burr's ghost does during these late-night walks, but it is clear that he prefers to time them for when everyone in the house is asleep.

A number of theories attempt to explain the nature of ghosts and the afterlife. Many experts believe that stressful events may leave behind an emotional imprint that takes on ghostly characteristics after the subject dies. Aaron Burr's ghost would certainly be a strong case for this theory. After killing one of the country's most prominent statesmen and becoming a wanted man in both New York and New Jersey, Aaron Burr spent what must have been the most difficult days of his life in the New Hope cellar.

Accustomed to the spirit's presence, the proprietors of the inn in the house built atop this old cellar named the establishment after the man who haunts it. "He's a playful kind of guy," Carl Glassman jokes as he speaks of Aaron Burr and his supernatural hijinks. The living, however, may never know if Burr shares the same insouciant outlook.

Baleroy Mansion

Located in the posh Philadelphia suburb of Chestnut Hill, Baleroy Mansion would probably speak if it could. The question is, what would it say? Given the foreboding air that surrounds it, perhaps the question best remains unanswered. If any house in America looks like it ought to be haunted, the sprawling Baleroy would be the one. Its architectural features include a mansard roof, ornamental cresting, an onion-domed turret and a pointed portico, as well as innumerable windows that stare out with a disturbing sentience. And although it is never wise to judge a book by its cover, in this case the stately mansion is actually every bit as haunted as its mysterious appearance suggests. Many paranormal experts, such as Charles J. Adams III, consider it one of the most haunted houses in Pennsylvania, if not the entire United States. Adams wrote an account of the haunting in his book *Philadelphia Ghost Stories*.

The house was built in 1911 and purchased 12 years later by the Easby family, in whose hands it has remained to this day. George Meade Easby—a direct descendant of

George Meade, the legendary general who commanded Union forces at the Battle of Gettysburg—has spent much of his life in the magnificent old mansion and has learned a lot about ghostly entities while living there. In fact, the elderly man's supernatural education began soon after his family moved into the house over 75 years ago.

The year was 1926, and six-year-old George was idly hunched over the fountain in the courtyard with his little brother, Steven. Both boys were staring at their rippling reflections with the kind of unwavering concentration unique to young children. In an instant, however, the clear waters in the Baleroy fountain revealed something that no young child should ever see. George could only stare in horrified silence as his brother's reflection suddenly changed. In place of the pensive expression of a thoughtful five-year-old child shimmered the image of a horrible grinning skull. Steven had been miraculously transformed into a skeleton.

The frightful image purling in the water might have receded from Mr. Easby's memory over the years were it not for the tragedy that soon followed. Not a month after George saw the skeleton in the fountain, Steven died. From that day onward, George knew in his heart that Baleroy Mansion was home to a supernatural presence.

The numerous events that occurred at Baleroy over subsequent years affirmed Mr. Easby's hunch. And although others were never able to get over the spooky phenomena that repeatedly went on in the house, George slowly grew accustomed to living alongside members of the netherworld, until ghosts became just another fact of what was to be a long and fascinating life.

Residents and nonresidents from all walks of life have had supernatural experiences in Baleroy Mansion. They've included psychics, skeptics, ministers, restoration workers and friends of the family. Many have had things thrown at them, heard strange noises or seen apparitions—in other words, the ghosts of Baleroy have spooked mortals in every way used by revenants throughout recorded history. One account tells how an encounter with one of the house's more malicious spirits led to the death of a Baleroy guest. With so many tales emerging from the mansion, where the dead seem to be more comfortable than the living, is it any wonder that the place is known as the most haunted building in Pennsylvania?

Many people would agree that Baleroy Mansion is an enviable place in which to live. With 33 resplendently furnished rooms, the extravagant estate emphasizes luxury. But unless the dead are able to enjoy material opulence, little explains the spirits' affinity for the place. Be they souls long gone or the recently deceased—we can only guess—the spirits of the deceased are inexplicably drawn to the mansion.

George's brother, Steven, had lived in the mansion for not even a year before he passed away, but numerous accounts confirm his continued presence. One involves restoration worker David Beltz, who, over the past 20 years, has been kept busy in the business of preservation at old Baleroy. Beltz and a co-worker were in the court-yard one day, working near the same fountain that had fascinated the Easby boys so many years ago. For no apparent reason, Beltz and his co-worker were seized by a sudden chill, as if Beethoven's Ninth Symphony was approaching its glorious conclusion.

Guided by something that can only be called instinct, both men looked up to the house, where they saw a young boy with bright blond hair staring down at them from the second floor. Beltz and his associate knew in their bones that they were not staring at a living person. An instant later, the boy vanished before their very eyes. The two found themselves staring through the now-empty window in amazed silence. "Man," Beltz's friend finally said, "that was just too strange." Based on Beltz's description, no one had any doubt that the boy was Steven Easby.

George Easby himself has had a number of experiences he would not be able to explain unless he invoked the ghost of his sibling. On one occasion, he was entertaining guests on his terrace when a loud crash was heard in the gallery. When the guests ran in to investigate, they found Steven's portrait lying face down on the floor. The painting had flung itself from the wall and flown about 15 feet through the air. What's more, the nail was still fastened to the wall and the wire on the frame was still taught, rendering what had just happened physically impossible. But somehow Mr. Easby was not surprised: he had known for a while that Steven's spirit had not left the house.

George attributes Steven's supernatural pranks to his mischievous nature when he was alive. Although George is sure that his brother never meant any harm to anyone, just like with any other attention-seeking boy, the lad's hijinks had to be disturbing enough to raise some eyebrows. In some instances, he may have gone too far. During another party, for example, Mr. Easby and some

20 others witnessed an ornamental copper pot fly across the room and connect with the side of a guest's head. The man was more surprised than hurt, but the bizarre and potentially dangerous event was enough to deter him from ever returning to Baleroy. Other spirits at Baleroy, however, are far more menacing than the prankish ghost of Steven Easby.

Once, George was awakened in the middle of the night by a moving weight on the edge of the bed, as if someone restless was sitting there. Before he realized that he was the only one in the house and no intruder alarms had gone off, an iron grip fastened around his arm, squeezing so tightly that it hurt. If he was tempted to entertain the idea that the event was just a dream, the deep bruises around his arm the next morning were solid enough evidence to the contrary.

Mr. Easby believes that the late night visitor was "Amanda," the most malicious ghost that haunts Baleroy Mansion. Considering how Paul Kimmons' meeting with this entity concluded, George might consider himself lucky for getting off with only a bruised arm. At the time of the encounter, Kimmons had worked for Mr. Easby for several years, and in all the time he had spent in Baleroy Mansion, he had never once laid eyes on a ghost. His general attitude toward the ghosts of Baleroy was skeptical, and it became habit to nod and smile politely whenever Mr. Easby or another visitor discussed the matter of spirits. His outlook was to change abruptly the day he saw the spirit of Amanda.

George had asked Kimmons to show a psychic named Judith Haimes through the house. On this tour, Kimmons saw Amanda for the first time. She appeared as a vague human form in the middle of a rolling blue mist, slowly drifting down the stairs toward Kimmons and Haimes before vanishing into thin air.

Haimes, a psychic and paranormal investigator, had seen this kind of thing before, and was not too shaken by the experience. But for Kimmons, the sight of the ghostly figure was too much for his rationalist sensibilities to absorb, and he never got over his encounter with the apparition. A few weeks later, Ms. Haimes received a disturbing phone call from Kimmons. His voice was tired and strained, and the psychic could tell that he was extremely distraught. He told Judith that the apparition on the stairs at Baleroy had somehow followed him home, and that he was seeing her almost daily. "I look in my rearview mirror and there she is, sitting in the back seat; I see her in the middle of a crowded street from the corner of my eye; I'll wake up in the middle of the night and see her standing there in front of my bed," he related.

Kimmons grew haggard as the month went on. The last time Mr. Easby saw his employee, the unlucky man was reclined in an antique chair in the study. He looked to be lost in a bad dream, fretfully twitching through a nervous sleep. A few days later, Kimmons was dead.

For Judith, Kimmons' death was directly related to the ghost they had both seen during her earlier investigation of the mansion. But as far as Mr. Easby was concerned, Kimmons was also the third man to die shortly after sitting in the chair in his study. He posted a sign to warn people against sitting in the chair, even cordoning it off with stanchions and velvet rope when he had guests. Paranormal enthusiasts who have studied Baleroy have no qualms about applying the sensational lexicon of their subculture to the chair in the study, and it has become widely knows as the "death chair" to those who are fascinated by it. Visitors are warned that they are taking their own lives in their hands if they sit in it.

As for Amanda, it's likely that she is somehow connected with the chair in the study because her mist-shrouded apparition has most often appeared in the room in question, hovering around the chair. She appears so often that the study has become known as the "Blue Room," and guests who fear run-ins with the spirit world avoid it. The predominant theory about the room is that Amanda occasionally materializes there before an unwary guest, hoping to lure him or her into the death chair.

Like Paul Kimmons, Lloyd Gross was a skeptic who spent a considerable amount of time in Baleroy. One of George Easby's closest friends and a fellow antique collector, Gross had grown accustomed to dismissing all the supernatural stories told about the house with a skeptical shrug—until, that is, the day his own two eyes fell on a sight that couldn't be accommodated by his level-headed belief system.

Gross was taking a reporter on a tour of Baleroy's antique treasures when the man's tape recorder practically leapt from his hand, sailed through the air and landed on the ground almost 20 feet away. Gross, assuming that the reporter had thrown his recorder into the air, looked at the man with wordless surprise, wondering what had provoked him to do such a thing. The reporter went cold with fear as he stuttered out his explanation. "Something pulled it out of my hand," was all the frazzled man could say. He was so shaken by the experience that they had to cut the tour short, and the reporter was sent home after being given a shot of whiskey to calm his nerves.

Whatever skepticism Lloyd Gross was able to maintain after the incident with the reporter rapidly dissolved upon his first encounter with Amanda. He was helping George prepare the house for a charity fundraiser when he saw the thick bluish mist drift out from the Blue Room. Even after the countless stories about Amanda's apparition and the fog that surrounded it, Gross instinctually looked for a rational explanation. "Look, it's getting cold out," he finally said to George, nodding in the direction of the Blue Room. George informed his friend that he wasn't looking at condensation but ectoplasm. Amanda was in the Blue Room.

The undeniable sight of Amanda's mist thoroughly spooked Lloyd Gross. Out of sorts for the rest of the night, Gross tried to ignore what he had seen earlier, but it was obvious to George that he was not able to do so. Mr. Easby could see the unease hovering just under his friend's eyes. Things got worse for Gross when the benefit was over. George was accompanying Lloyd to his car when, for no apparent reason, his spooked friend suddenly spun around to face him. New fear arose in Gross' eyes. "Why did you hit me?" he asked of his surprised host.

Both men knew the question was absurd; George had been standing over 10 feet away from where Gross was. "I didn't hit you," Mr. Easby responded, "I'm way over here."

After all those years of no contact, the spirits of Baleroy had decided to visit Lloyd Gross twice in one night. But they weren't content to stop there. For when he arrived home later that evening, through his front window he could see smoke billowing in his foyer. Certain that his house was on fire, he bolted to the door and threw it open, only to see the blue fog instantly dissipate around him. His heart froze in a debilitating fear when he realized that whatever he had seen in Baleroy had followed him home. Gross would never doubt the ghosts of Baleroy ever again.

As frightening as people's experiences with Amanda have been, Mr. Easby maintains that the benevolent spirits far outnumber those bent on making trouble. For instance, Mr. Easby saw an apparition of his deceased uncle on more than one occasion. Other apparitions have also made appearances. One that bears a striking resemblance to Thomas Jefferson has been seen hovering next to a tall clock in the dining room. An image of an elderly lady doubled over with a cane in her hand has been spotted in the second-floor hallway. Recurring reports also indicate a smiling monk in brown robes who appears out of nowhere in the master bedroom on the second floor. Nothing about these encounters has disturbed the patriarch of Baleroy Mansion in the slightest.

A particularly interesting ghost is the kind and protective spirit of George Easby's mother, Henrietta. Not only did she attempt to reach across the wall between the living and the dead to express her motherly affections, but the genteel Victorian lady also took an active part in her son's life, revealing more than one unseen family treasure collecting dust in the old mansion.

Henrietta often communicated through Judith Haimes, the same psychic who was standing next to Paul Kimmons the fateful moment he first set eyes on Amanda. Ms. Haimes was driving to Baleroy for dinner one evening when she received her first message from Henrietta. The psychic became aware of a woman's voice, muttering the same word over and over again: "Longfellow, Longfellow, Longfellow…"

Unsure what the voice meant, she did not say anything to Mr. Easby during dinner, even though the voice persisted for the whole meal. When the voice added the phrase "the children's hour" to its previous mantra, Judith finally asked Mr. Easby if he knew what any of it meant. George was struck speechless. After a long silence, he spoke up. "Henry Wadsworth Longfellow was my mother's favorite poet," he explained to Ms. Haimes, "and 'The Children's Hour' was her favorite poem."

George was in his study later that evening, trying to forget what had transpired during supper by losing himself in a book. He quickly noticed that one book was jutting out from the shelf, as if someone had thought reading it would be a good idea, began to pull it out, then thought twice and left it there. Getting up to slide the book back in place, George froze when he saw the name on the spine: Henry Wadsworth Longfellow.

With trembling hands, he reached up to where the volume sat on the big oak shelf and pulled it down. It was dusty—obviously untouched for many years—and the edge of an old yellowed envelope jutted from the top of the book, marking a page within. George slowly opened the volume of poetry to the page flagged by the envelope. Sure enough, it opened to his mother's favorite poem, "The Children's Hour." On the envelope, in his mother's elegantly flowing longhand, was written, "To my son Meade in the event of my death." With baited breath, George picked up the envelope and folded its top back. The mystery only deepened when he looked inside; there was nothing at all inside the envelope. It was empty.

From that day onward, Henrietta began to correspond with her son through Judith Haimes fairly regularly. Ms. Haimes was made aware of two silver candlesticks that Henrietta had hidden in the rafters of a long-forgotten storeroom. Mr. Easby was thrilled when Judith led the way to a secret drawer concealed in one of the house's old desks. Hidden there was a bullet-ridden and powder-burnt Confederate flag that had been captured at the Battle of Gettysburg. Over the next few weeks, family secrets began to come out of the woodwork.

The most dramatic family heirloom uncovered was in the attic. Acting with supernaturally endowed intelligence, Ms. Haimes opened one of the countless trunks stored there and, after rummaging for a brief time, emerged with a single document. She held an ancient promissory note in her hand, dating back to the early 19th century. The paper revealed that George's great-great-grandfather, Richard Meade, had lent the federal government five million dollars in 1819 to cover the debts incurred by the United States in its annexation of Spanish Florida. Apparently, the Easby family had never been reimbursed. In 1990, based on the information provided by his mother through

Ms. Haimes, George Easby made a formal demand to the state of Florida for the five million dollars, plus all interest accumulated in the 170 years since. Whether he will get the money or not is still in question.

For reasons unknown, Henrietta communicated less frequently with Ms. Haimes after she revealed the existence of the promissory note. In one of her last psychic transmissions, she disclosed another message from the past. This time, however, it hit a little closer to home. It was a letter from George's father, M. Stevenson Easby, a hard-headed agnostic who had scoffed at any suggestion of the supernatural—or so George had thought.

The letter revealed that George's father had been aware of the ghosts in Baleroy for most of his life, and his rigid pragmatism was only a front for the sake of his child. It seems that the senior Easby would admit the existence of ghosts to his son only after he himself had become one. In the letter to George, intended to be read after he had died, M. Stevenson admitted that he had indeed seen the ghosts. Yet he assured his son that there was nothing to be afraid of, that the ghosts of Baleroy could do no harm if he did not let them.

Perhaps this final message from his stoic father imbued George Easby with the strength to accept his haunted home as gracefully as he does. In fact, Mr. Easby not only accepts the ghosts in his mansion, he relishes their being there. He has no qualms about taking paranormal enthusiasts on tours through the mansion, and the fame Baleroy has acquired in the paranormal community is no doubt partly the result of his willingness to let others partake of Baleroy's ghosts.

2
Ghosts of the Past

~

Though the past is always receding in time, it never really goes away. Just as we as individuals are shaped largely by our past experiences, so too does our society exist as an evolution of ideas and action over time. What is our culture but an accumulation of the general beliefs, assumptions and popular expressions that have developed over the course of our history?

The idea that "past is present," however, takes on a completely different meaning where Pennsylvania's supernatural legends are concerned. For woven into the tumultuous history of the state are a number of ghostly tales that have survived over time. What sets the stories in the following chapter apart from the rest of the book is their historical backdrop, set in times and places central to what Pennsylvania was and is today. Not only are these ghostly beings rooted in significant events of the state's history, but sightings of them continue to be reported to this very day—a solid, if unsettling, demonstration of how the past repeatedly comes back to haunt us.

~

Gettysburg

Before the Civil War, little about Gettysburg distinguished it from any other small municipal settlement in Pennsylvania. Relying largely on agricultural activity for subsistence, the town was best known for its position at the hub of six highways. This humble claim to fame changed after the events of July 1, 1863. That morning, two Confederate brigades, tired, hungry and badly in need of supplies, crested Herr Ridge, a promontory overlooking the sleeping town.

Brigadier Generals James Archer and Joseph David had no idea they were initiating the deciding battle of the Civil War when they ordered their units to occupy the town. The Union forces defending Gettysburg put up what resistance they could against the advancing Confederates, and they spent much of that fateful morning staging a fighting withdrawal from the superior numbers on the Southern side. The scale of the engagement increased dramatically as the Confederates pushed through the streets of Gettysburg. Reinforcements from both sides continued to arrive as the day wore on, with the last soldiers marching into the area just before midnight. The next morning saw General Robert E. Lee's entire Army of Northern Virginia, 75,000 strong, arrayed just south of Gettysburg, glaring across at General George G. Meade's 97,000-man Army of the Potomac.

By then, it was obvious that something terrible was about to happen. And it did. From July 1 to July 3, the roaring machinery of the Civil War claimed over 50,000 American lives, making Gettysburg the bloodiest battle of the four-year conflict. In fact, measured by the sad scales of human tragedy, the losses incurred at Gettysburg dwarf those of any other battle in American history. Although the United States military has weathered more than one tragedy since its inception, the horrors of Antietam, Pearl Harbor or D-Day taken individually do not match, by sheer volume, the unforgiving brutality of Gettysburg.

Given the bloodshed, is it any wonder that Gettysburg is considered the most haunted place in the United States? If a single untimely death can cause a disgruntled spirit to haunt an area for years, what happens when tens of thousands lose their lives in the staggering horror of battle? It could be the sheer trauma of the events leading up to death or the lasting acrimony of those soldiers reluctant to give their own lives for abstract political ideals. Perhaps it was the deep historical significance of soldiers' actions as they marched over the battlefield during those three days. Whatever the case, Gettysburg today is filled with the spirits of men who fought—and died—there well over 100 years ago.

Among all the ghostly occurrences that have been witnessed in National Military Park, the supernatural sightings on Little Round Top and at the Devil's Den have received the most attention. Not surprisingly, it is around these two locations near the southernmost limits of the site that much of the battle's most critical combat took place.

Little Round Top, a forested hill that loomed over the Union line's left flank, was a valuable strategic location for both the Confederate forces and the Union Army. If the Confederates were able to take the high ground on Little Round Top, their elevated position over the Union lines

Little Round Top, the site of a decisive Gettysburg engagement, is also the focus of much unexplained paranormal activity.

could shatter General Meade's entire flank and secure victory for the rebels. Therefore, it would seem imperative to the Union strategy that its left flank be anchored with a strong defensive position on Little Round Top. But the Union command had initially overlooked the importance of the hill and had left it virtually unoccupied, instead positioning the left flank army on rocky ground near the base of Little Round Top—a boulder-strewn stretch of land known as the Devil's Den.

It was at the Devil's Den that the Confederate attack on the Union's left flank began. The fighting for the

Devil's Den was fierce and bloody, raging back and forth for much of the day. Sharpshooters nesting behind the massive boulders traded lead with each other as lines of infantry advanced, took over, retreated and then advanced again over the now-bloody outcropping of rocks. The see-saw battle ended with the Stars and Bars waving over the Devil's Den, and with thousands of battered and bloodied men from Georgia and Texas standing among nearly as many dead.

The legendary assault on Little Round Top began soon after the Confederates attacked the Devil's Den. Union command became aware of the imminent danger Little Round Top posed to their position when a Union engineer on lookout became suspicious of the hill's heavily wooded southern slope. Ordering a shell to be fired into the area, he was startled to see the sudden gleam of countless gun barrels and bayonets. There was no mistaking what he saw in the trees—an enormous body of Confederate infantry poised to make the ascent up the suddenly strategically critical hill.

Immediately aware of what this Confederate move would mean to the Union position, the officer relayed a desperate message to General Meade, who ordered the hill be defended at once. Brigadier General James Barnes arrived at Little Round Top just in time to greet the advancing Confederates, inaugurating what would become one of the decisive engagements of Gettysburg with a devastating volley of rifle fire. The enormous losses suffered on both sides over the next few hours would transform Little Round Top from an anonymous hill rising out of the farmlands of southern Pennsylvania into a site of massive carnage.

Wave after wave of Confederate soldiers rushed up the murderous slope only to be repulsed by the shrinking line of Union men at the top. The hardest-pressed regiment holding the crest of Little Round Top was the 20th Maine, led by the now-legendary Colonel Joshua Chamberlain. The 386 men in Chamberlain's unit guarded the southernmost tip of the entire Army of the Potomac. Just before Chamberlain's superior officer galloped off to supervise the rest of the defense, he reminded the colonel of his incredible responsibility: "You understand. You are to hold this ground at all costs."

The regiment's onerous duty to protect the left flank was made even more difficult by the 15th Alabama, who were charging up the hill and constantly threatening to outflank them. Stretched thin and running out of powder, the 20th Maine held off one charge after another, repeatedly sending the Alabama rebels into a retreat toward the base of the hill, where they would regroup and come again. As the 20th Maine's casualties mounted and their ammunition dwindled, Colonel Chamberlain gave the order that would win him the Medal of Honor.

"Fix bayonets!" the colonel yelled over the roar of gunfire and cannon blasts.

Although it seemed hard to believe, every soldier along the line knew that their situation was about to get worse. Their colonel intended to order them out from behind their covered positions to charge the Confederates below. That was precisely what he did. In the next moment, the seemingly suicidal command came down the line: "Charge!"

For an instant, it seemed as if the 20th would not be able to carry out this order as the regiment balked before the

This monument commemorates the courage of those who fought—and died—at Little Round Top.

sight of the Alabaman regiment below. But the bravery of a single lieutenant challenged the courage of each and every man at the top of the hill. Obeying the command without any hesitation, the man charged down the slope alone. A few seconds later, the 20th Maine was surging forward right behind him, rushing down the southern slope of Little Round Top, Colonel Chamberlain leading the way. No one there had any way of knowing it at the time, but the redoubtable Chamberlain was leading them to glory.

The suddenly aggressive move caught the Confederate regiment completely off guard, and they reeled under the onslaught of the surprise counterattack. After a few harried moments of hand-to-hand combat, the Alabama regiment broke, retreating from the hill with the sound of the cheering Union men behind them. Colonel Chamberlain and the 20th Maine had saved the Union flank.

The extraordinary counterattack of the New England regiment that day was matched only by the extraordinary scope of the slaughter. Dead men, both Union and Confederate, were littered across the Devil's Den. The narrow gulch that dipped down between that rocky battlefield and Little Round Top was so choked with the bodies of fallen soldiers that it became known as the Valley of Death from that day onward. And the slopes of Little Round Top itself were virtually blanketed by the bodies of the slain.

The Confederate attempt on the Union left had been thwarted. The next day, the hottest fighting moved north along the line. A few weeks after that, all that was left in the area were memories of the brutality of that July day— memories that were determined not to be forgotten.

It is difficult to say who saw the first ghosts around Little Round Top. One popular legend has the men of the 20th Maine spotting the spirit of none other than George Washington on the day of the battle. According to this tale, it was the sight of his bold image, standing before the regiment's line with sword raised toward the enemy, that inspired the wavering men to make their daring attack down the side of Little Round Top.

Whether or not the spirit of George Washington would be so roused by the fighting as to return from the grave and lead the beleaguered men of the 20th into battle is open to speculation. But as romantic as the supernatural legend is, there are no surviving firsthand accounts of veterans claiming to have seen the towering first president leading them forward with a raised sword. Certainly no one since the battle of Gettysburg has said anything about a specter of George Washington brandishing a sword at Little Round Top.

Although George Washington seems to have retreated quietly back into his grave, it seems that many of the men who died on the southern reaches of the greatest Civil War battle have been unable to find their own resting places.

All sorts of bizarre incidents have been reported around Little Round Top over the years. Many visitors to the National Military Park who have lingered on the hill late into the day have been treated to eerie displays. During the early hours of clear, cloudless nights, thick mists can suddenly form around the hill, rising in thick tendrils from the ground where thousands fell. From within this thick fog, people standing at the top of the hill may witness long lines of numerous flashing lights coming to life on the terrain below. They report that these lights do not flash only once, nor do they remain still. In fact, the flashes continue at regular intervals, starting small, as if coming from a distance, and getting slightly larger with each consecutive illumination. By the time the lights flash for the final time, they appear to be no more than 30 yards from the witnesses at the summit of Little Round Top—and then they are gone. Although no one can say for sure, most people believe that this recurring phenomenon is a supernatural reenactment of the Confederate advance on Little Round Top.

On other occasions, people have spotted a transparent horseman dressed in a Union officer's uniform astride a phantom steed. The horse picks its way down the side of the hill with slow, careful steps—as if the ghostly beast is conscious that the officer on its back is headless and unable to choose a path for himself.

One of the most frequently occurring phenomena in the area of the battle involves cameras. Gettysburg being the popular tourist destination that it is, millions of people with cameras of every type have descended on it at one time or another, snapping pictures or recording videos of the famous battleground. Although some mechanical difficulties would certainly be expected given the number of people who have visited, the natures of some of the malfunctions have been a little too freakish to be casually disregarded.

Many visitors have found that their cameras have inexplicably jammed up when they tried capturing certain areas on camera. This especially seems to happen in places where there were particularly high concentrations of casualties. Brand-new cameras have mysteriously stopped working when used to take pictures of the Valley of Death, where countless Confederate soldiers fell during the assaults on the Devil's Den and Little Round Top. Many people attempting to take pictures here have their cameras simply freeze up—film won't load, shutters won't open or batteries will go dead. Whereas many of these individuals get angry that their equipment is not functioning, others claim to feel a cold, uncomfortable feeling, as if they aren't welcome in the spot where they're standing. Just as this feeling always subsides when the person walks away from

A 19th-century drawing of the dramatic events in the Devil's Den

the area, so too does the previously faulty equipment suddenly begin to work again.

Out among the massive boulders of Devil's Den, a completely different type of camera-related phenomenon has been said to occur. Tourists looking for the perfect shot to tuck into their photo albums have reported the appearance of a scraggly looking young man, barefoot and dressed in patched-up clothing, with a big floppy hat sitting atop his long brown hair. Speaking with a thick Southern drawl, he often gives photographic advice to people who are puzzling over shadow and light. "There's yer shot," he'll say, pointing toward one cluster of boulders. People who can't seem to choose what area deserves preservation on film often turn around to find themselves face-to-face with this young man. "How 'bout them rocks over there?" he suggests helpfully.

The advice he gives is almost always taken, but when the photographers turn to thank the young man for his help, they are surprised to see that he has disappeared as quickly and quietly as he came. Park managers have heard more than one inquiry about the "helpful young hippie in the Devil's Den."

Some tourists have no opportunity to mistake this man for a free-spirited flower child. They are the ones who first notice him when looking through their recently developed photographs of the battlefield. He appears in the pictures of the Devil's Den, sometimes faintly, sometimes much more discernibly, staring blankly at the photographer. Long hair, big hat, roughly clothed and barefoot—what shocks most people about the appearance of this lone celluloid image is that he wasn't there when the picture was taken.

This man has come to be recognized as the Confederate ghost of the Devil's Den. Why he has chosen to stay behind is anybody's guess, and why he seems to have taken an interest in the art of photography is just as mysterious. Perhaps he was a man who once had a deep appreciation for the landscape and has remained behind in Devil's Den to help others capture the natural beauty of the place. Or maybe he was one of those whose death came so suddenly and so violently that some part of his soul is unable to recognize that he is gone, so he still hangs around the site of his demise, making himself useful any way he can.

Another ghost is related to one of the more recognizable Gettysburg battlefield photos, probably taken by

Timothy O'Sullivan, who was among the first photographers to arrive after the battle was over. A young Confederate soldier lies dead in a sharpshooter's nest tucked within the huge boulders of Devil's Den. The poignancy of the picture lies in the clarity of the details. Whoever the Confederate is, his facial features stand out clearly enough to distinguish him from many of the other faceless dead that were captured by Civil War photographers. While decomposition has just begun to swell his clean-shaven face, we can still see an exhausted death grimace on his face. His weapon is propped against the stone wall he would have been shooting from behind; an open cartridge box lies next to him. Was he reloading his rifle when he was shot? His unbuttoned jacket, perhaps a few sizes too big, is worn over a ruffled white shirt. Did he undo his jacket in the heat of battle? Or perhaps he tried yanking his shirt off in the last moments of his life in a vain attempt to see the wound that claimed him. These are just some of the questions casual observers might ask themselves when looking at this dramatic study of a man's last moments.

That is before they are informed of the details behind the photograph. For it turns out that Timothy O'Sullivan was more interested in dramatic effect than he was in accuracy. Deeply affected by his deceased subject, O'Sullivan had the body moved from another part of the battlefield and carefully placed among the rocks of Devil's Den, along with the rifle and cartridge box. So it is that the photograph is as much a study of a man's last moments as it is of another man's determination to take a good picture.

During a visit to the battlefield, one witness saw a man matching the description of the fallen soldier in this famous photograph.

While the facts behind the picture are familiar to many Civil War buffs, it remains one of the definitive photographs taken after the battle of Gettysburg. A woman named "Allison," who prefers to go by a pseudonym, has only seen the picture a few times, but the dead young man has become synonymous with the horrible Civil War battle for her. "I'm not such a big Civil War buff myself," Allison says, "but on occasion I flip through my husband, 'Jack's,' books. That picture has always struck me as especially sad. He looks so young; it makes me wonder about how many boys were killed during that battle. I wonder what they were thinking when they died."

Allison's husband is an ardent Civil War enthusiast, and the couple have spent more than one family vacation at Gettysburg, walking among the numerous monuments on the battlefield. Allison says she just tends to look around at the other people while Jack becomes lost in silence, trying to absorb the significance of the location or the chaos that transpired there so long ago. "Sometimes Jack will talk about some detail of the battle, but for the most part, we just walk around. There are always a few people dressed up in period costumes."

During their last visit to Gettysburg, in the summer of 2000, Allison took notice of one young visitor who was dressed up in such a costume near the base of Little Round Top. Something about his costume seemed too real. "It's just that I've never seen a period costume look so old before," Allison says. "It looked dirty and worn, and the cuffs were threadbare." But Allison was even more struck by the young man's demeanor. "His face was completely expressionless. He was just standing there looking at the peak of Little Round Top, like he was oblivious to everyone around him. In the minute or so I was watching him, he didn't blink once." But what disturbed Allison most about the young man was how oddly familiar he was. She wasn't sure where she had seen him before, but she was certain that she had.

Thinking that he might be one of their children's friends, she tapped Jack on the shoulder, intending to tell him about the strange youngster, but when she turned back to where he was standing, there was no one there.

"I was completely shocked; I can't ever remember feeling that way. My heart was pounding like a drum and my stomach got all topsy-turvy. I thought I was going to faint." She looked so distraught that Jack got worried and led her to one of the big boulders in Devil's Den, where they sat down. By the time Allison got her bearings back, Jack felt comfortable enough to joke about the incident. "Well, maybe he was a ghost. You know what they say— this place is supposed to be full of 'em."

Though she laughed, those words stuck with Allison for a long time after. Almost a year later, she made the shocking discovery that answered the nagging questions she had been asking herself during quiet moments. "Jack was off fishing, and I was just sitting around with a cup of tea, flipping through one of his Civil War books, mostly just looking at the pictures." She let out a little scream when her eyes fell on the dead sharpshooter in Devil's Den. "I was so startled I dropped my cup on the floor. It was him. I swear it—that was the boy I saw on the battlefield that day. It suddenly all made sense to me, and even though I was scared, I was also somehow relieved. I mean, I wasn't going crazy after all."

Allison did not reveal her discovery to her husband, and doesn't plan on telling him any time soon. "I don't think he would take the news very well," she says today. "I doubt he'd believe me, and he thinks I'm crazy enough as it is." In fact, Allison hasn't told a soul about the dead Confederate soldier she believes she saw in Gettysburg that day. But after doing a little research on the man in the picture, she says that she isn't so surprised that his soul lingers on the battlefield. "They shouldn't have used the poor man's remains that way," Allison says. "I don't think he's happy that they made a show of his dead body. I think that's why he's still there, standing on the spot where he was really killed."

The ghosts described here are just a small sample of the paranormal activity that goes on in Gettysburg. From the bloody ground of the infamous Angle to the legendary Wheatfield, numerous revenants have been sighted over the years. In a sense, we can only expect as much. Given the staggering loss of life that occurred around this once-innocent little Pennsylvania town, we can only expect that such devastation might leave an impression on the place. With all the monuments, reenactments and history lessons that center on it, the living have continued to recognize the immense sacrifice that took place on the battlefield. As for the dead, it seems that they too are intent on making sure that people don't forget what happened during the first three days of July 1863. And odds are that visitors to the Gettysburg National Military Park—possibly the most haunted place in North America—will have a better chance of witnessing a supernatural phenomenon than they would anywhere else on the continent.

Mad Anthony Wayne

He is one of Pennsylvania's favorite sons: General Anthony Wayne, the 18th-century Revolutionary War hero who gave over 20 of his 51 years in staunch service to the United States. He was both a fearless soldier whose heart thrilled in the chaos of battle and a careful general who never made command decisions without proper deliberation. But above all, Wayne was gifted with an amazing knack at pulling off major victories when the people of the fledgling United States most needed them. And although countless individuals threw their lives into building the young country, there were few who could boast such stunning success at repulsing America's enemies as could this Pennsylvania-born general.

Anthony Wayne's name probably doesn't figure largely in the lives of most Pennsylvanians today, but the general's legacy is apparent on any map of the state. In addition to the municipalities of Wayne, Waynesboro and Waynesburg, nine townships and one county bear his name. For those who choose not to believe in an afterlife, such widespread posthumous recognition may be considered as close to immortality as an individual can get.

According to the following tale, however, a person can achieve an entirely different sort of immortality, regardless of place names and legendary acclaim. In addition to Wayne's name being spread across the state, one might say that so are his very remains: some of the general is respectfully buried in the state's northwest corner, in Presque Isle, while other parts are quietly resting in the southeast corner, in the small hamlet of Radnor in

Chester County. The rest of him is scattered somewhere between. Such an unorthodox state of postmortem affairs—in addition to an untimely death at the peak of his career—might impel the spirit of Anthony Wayne to haunt the state that bred him.

Wayne was born in Radnor on January 1, 1745. Not much about his early life indicated that he achieve the status of a living legend. The only thing that really stood out about young Wayne was his fervent love for all matters military. A mediocre student, he owed most of his opportunities to the favors of patronage and his family's lofty social standing. After a failed attempt at land surveying while he was in his early 20s, he returned to Radnor to work with his father, helping with the family farm and tannery. At the time, enthusiasm and influence were enough to make one an officer in the Continental Army. On January 3, 1776, Wayne was commissioned as colonel of the Fourth Pennsylvania Battalion. It would prove to be the start of a long and illustrious military career.

He distinguished himself as one of the revolution's pre-eminent military figures, capable of molding any group of men into a premier fighting force. Although cautious with his strategies, the dauntless general was not reluctant to join the front lines and roar in the face of the enemy. This tendency to revel in the physical dangers of battle earned him the sobriquet "Mad" Anthony Wayne, one of the more illustrious names to go down in the annals of American history.

On his first battle command, Wayne's battalion covered the retreat of the American Army out of Canada after the

Some of Anthony Wayne's remains are interred in this plot outside St. David's Church in Radnor.

Battle of Three Rivers. Promoted to brigadier general following his command of Fort Ticonderoga, Wayne fought next at Brandywine Creek, where he held back the British Army while Washington and his defeated force retreated to safety. Remaining in the thick of the action throughout the rest of the war, Anthony Wayne was already a famous officer when he won his illustrious victory at Stony Point.

The legendary attack took place on July 16, 1779. That evening, Mad Anthony personally led a bayonet attack on the British fort. The general was grazed by a musket shot during the approach and had to be carried over the parapet by his men. Nevertheless, he remained in command of his unit until the battle was over, bellowing orders over the clash of combat as the American soldiers captured the fort's flag and took over 500 British prisoners. Stony Point was a major morale boost for the revolution, which had until then won too few military victories against the British Army. After the colonies won their independence, the war hero returned to civilian life.

But just as it was before the war, Wayne was less successful in civilian life than he was in the military. After a failed attempt at running a plantation in Georgia and a number of botched political endeavors, Mad Anthony considered himself lucky that sufficient unrest on the continent still required a man of his abilities. Hostile American Indians and a persistent British presence west of the Ohio River impelled George Washington to create a standing American Army. Anthony Wayne was chosen as the commander-in-chief of the country's first army.

On August 20, 1794, Wayne led the Legion of the United States to a resounding victory at the Battle of Fallen Timbers, defeating the war chief Little Turtle and the Miami Confederacy that had assembled under him. Like a victorious Caesar returning from Gaul, Mad Anthony Wayne was at the peak of his career when he rode back into Pennsylvania in the winter of 1796. Some historians claim that his popularity was such that even the title of president was within his reach. Of this we can never be certain, though. On his way back to Pittsburgh, he became seriously ill. He would never beat the illness. Whatever ambitions he entertained died with him along the shores of Lake Erie. He passed away in the recently constructed blockhouse and was given a soldier's burial under the flagpole. So passed away one of America's greatest.

But his story does not end there. Thirteen years later, Wayne's son, Isaac, made the trip from Chester County to Erie with the intent of taking his father's remains back to the family plot in Radnor. Everyone involved in exhuming the general's corpse must have been shocked and dismayed when they discovered that his body was remarkably well preserved. Isaac was understandably unwilling to transport the rotting corpse of his father across the state in the back of his wagon. Instead, he consulted a doctor, who recommended that the remains be boiled in a caldron, thus separating the dead general's bones from his tissue.

Isaac followed the doctor's advice. The fleshy remains of Mad Anthony Wayne that were left in the bottom of the pot were once again buried in Erie. The general's bones, unfortunately, had no such luck. Legend has it that a good number them were jolted from the wagon on the way back. As Isaac made his way down what is now U.S. Route 322, the wagon lifted and swung over the rocky, heavily rutted road, leaving a rough trail of the general's bones from Erie to Radnor. After a ceremony in St. David's Church in Radnor on July 4, 1809, what was left of Wayne's skeleton was buried in the family plot.

According to countless eyewitnesses, however, the hero's rest has not been a peaceful one. Every New Year's

Day since his burial, an apparition of the dead general has been spotted along Route 322, mounted on a phantom horse. The figure tears down the highway at an incredible speed, passing straight through anything in its way without breaking stride. Some eyewitnesses have been able to make out the details of his uniform—the epaulets on his shoulders, his saber bouncing at his side and his tricorne hat sitting atop his powdered wig.

The same people have also reported that his blank eyes glance from one side of the road to the other, almost as if to search for something that is lying on the side of the highway. Such accounts give credence to the popular theory that Mad Anthony's ghost is looking for the bones that were not buried with him in Radnor. In this scenario, the apparition reflects Wayne's supernatural discontent at having his remains disturbed and strewn across the state.

Other theories also exist. A few of his biographers write about how difficult it must have been for the headstrong general to face such a meek end so soon after winning glory on the battlefield. If Mad Anthony Wayne had his choice, he would surely have preferred to fall in a hail of musket fire than in the quiet comfort of an Erie blockhouse. His last breaths must have brought with them the realization that had his frail mortal frame not failed him, his victory at Fallen Timbers may have cast him into the highest echelons of society, perhaps even as far as the presidency. The world was finally his oyster, but he could not even get out of bed. Those who shudder at the thought of such frustrated ambition are more inclined to believe that Mad Anthony's apparition is a result of the general's anger at never being able to enjoy the fruits of his labors.

Either way, drivers on U.S. Route 322 on New Year's Day should beware. Unless you don't mind having a 200-year-old ghost pass straight through your car, it would be wise to give any ghostly horseman in the rearview mirror the right of way.

Tate House

The Hessian soldiers who crossed the Atlantic in 1776 are the outsiders of American history. They were Germans who were enlisted in the British Army and were brought overseas to prevent the formation of the United States. Recruited by the losing side, they fought in a conflict they had no vested interest in, and their German tongues did not even allow them to communicate with either their allies or their enemies. It was neither their fight nor their land— they were outsiders in the truest sense of the word.

The War of Independence ran its well-documented course, during which these outsiders did all they could to meet the demands of duty and survival. Their fortunes varied from man to man. Many of them went back home after the struggle in America was over. Some of the Hessians found something on the continent that they could call familiar and ended up settling down in the young nation after the fighting. Others succumbed to darker fates, dying on battlefields far from home. And then there were the other Hessians, those few hapless men doomed to even greater misfortune than their fallen comrades, men whose souls could never overcome the tragic circumstances of their deaths. Their spirits are damned to relive the tragedy of their earthly days, long after their days on this earth have expired.

Of all the ghostly figures that are reported to drift across Pennsylvania's paranormal landscape, the pale, glimmering images of Hessian specters are the ones that appear most often. Whether the phantom mercenaries appear as headless manifestations, stare out of hanging portraits with disturbing sentience or aimlessly wander through old graveyards at night, these displaced casualties of the American Revolution appear determined to leave a supernatural impression on the strange land they fought in so many years ago.

George School is a prestigious Quaker boarding school in Newtown, Bucks County. At first glance, nothing about the institution suggests that anything unusual might be happening here. The noisy halls, quiet classrooms and capable teachers lend George School's campus an academic air that might be found in any one of the country's secondary schools. But a dark story lies under George School's predictable days of regimented instruction. According to local legend, the spirit of a long-dead Hessian haunts one of the oldest buildings on campus.

Today, Tate House is used for teachers' quarters, but it was not always so. The big stone structure was built in the 18th century, long before George School was founded. It used to be the home of wealthy colonist Anthony Tate, who passed it on to his son, James, upon his death in 1781. James Tate acted as a surgeon in the Continental Army during the War of Independence, and

Paranormal activity at Tate House is connected to Dr. James Tate's unusual scientific dissections.

he became a devoted medical practitioner after the fighting was over. He made his basement into a primitive laboratory, dedicating many of his daylight hours in the candlelit darkness of his cellar to the taking apart of whatever organism he could find in order to further his knowledge of biology.

Pigs, dogs, horses, chickens—Dr. James Tate gleaned what knowledge he could from his subterranean dissections, but his pursuit of knowledge could only go so far if he limited himself to farm animals; what he yearned for was human study. It was a time, however, when the idea of donating one's remains to advance the progress of scientific study was not so readily accepted by the general population. His neighbors already discussed what they thought was the man's disconcerting behavior in suspicious whispers. Some spied him dragging dead animals into the darkness of his cellar; others caught him hauling huge bloodstained sacks out into his field and burying them. Studying dead animals was strange enough, so who knows what people would have thought if they were to find out that Dr. Tate was also dissecting human corpses in his basement?

As mindful as he was of what his neighbors might think, Dr. Tate was determined to examine human anatomy. He learned that a Hessian prisoner of war who had been detained in Newtown had died recently, and his body had just been buried in a cemetery outside of town. On a dark and moonless night, the surgeon took one of his carriages out to the cemetery. He dug up the dead soldier's body, loaded it into his carriage and took it back to his cellar laboratory.

He dissected the corpse by candlelight for the next several nights, drawing intricate diagrams and taking painstaking notes on everything he found. Unwilling to take the corpse outside after he was done, Dr. Tate buried what was left of the Hessian in the dirt of his cellar floor. Soon afterward, strange things began to happen at Tate House—irregular events that would upset the empirical rationalism at the heart of Dr. Tate's medical studies.

The most common occurrence that took place in the cellar would be the mysteriously extinguished candles. Whenever Tate would walk over the area where he had buried the Hessian, the candle he was holding would go out. No draft had wafted through the room, and he had done nothing himself to snuff out the light. Nevertheless, the candle he held would suddenly go out without fail whenever he stood over the burial site of his Hessian study, leaving him in the pitch darkness of his suddenly freezing room.

The phenomenon repeated itself so often that Dr. Tate took to walking around the slight elevation in his cellar floor. As soon as he had made this adjustment, even stranger things began to happen. He would hear footsteps in the middle of the night, slow and heavy, making their way up the cellar steps and onto the ground floor of his home. The master of the house would get up from bed, light a candle and make the rounds through his home. He never found anyone there. A few times, his searches would take him down into his cellar, where he would repeatedly find no corporeal intruder. But when he walked over the Hessian's remains, his candle would instantly go out, and a deep unearthly cold would freeze the surgeon to his very bones.

Dr. Tate eventually passed away, but the cold presence averse to light remained in his cellar, terrorizing subsequent inhabitants of Tate House. More than one person has told of the heavy footsteps moving up the cellar steps and walking slowly through the halls on the first floor. The stories have persisted to this very day, and teachers at George School who have lived in the house have experienced strange phenomena that cannot be rationally explained.

One mathematics instructor reported chronic difficulties with the basement heater's pilot light. Every now and then, the pilot light in the heater would just go out. The furnace was replaced, but that did not help; the heater's light would still go off for no explicable reason. The school called in furnace repair technicians to take a look, but they could come up with no explanation either. By all indications, Tate House's new heater should have been working fine.

The presence in the cellar did not limit its activity to small flames. When the school had one of the walls in the house painted, strange scratches and long cracks appeared in the fresh paint soon after it had dried. And then there were the noises. Teachers have heard the legendary footsteps late in the night. The same noises as reported before: plodding footsteps making their way up from the cellar and through the halls of the old house, as if some heavy sleepwalker was looking for something in a confused dream. Whenever anyone went down to investigate, there was never anybody there.

Although there have been no actual sightings of the Hessian in Tate House, the annals of local ghost lore have long accepted that the spirit of the dead German soldier is responsible for the eerie goings-on there. Certainly the last years of the Hessian's life were turbulent enough to account for a restless spirit after death. Dislocated from his home in Europe, taken prisoner in a foreign war to ultimately die in captivity—it is not too hard to imagine how difficult the man's life must have been in his latter years. Even after he was buried, there was no rest for the rootless Hessian. Disturbed in his grave by the ambitious James Tate, the foreigner had even his remains uprooted, laid on a surgeon's operating table and unceremoniously carved up. Although the Hessian's name is forever lost to history, his spirit seems intent on remaining in residence at Tate House.

The Ghosts of Fort Mifflin

The American struggle for independence wasn't going so well in the fall of 1777. George Washington's Continental Army was in full retreat after the British victory at the Battle of Brandywine, leaving General William Howe free to march into Philadelphia. The famous British general was poised to deal the deathblow to Washington's defeated soldiers, who were camped just west of the city. Lacking only adequate supplies, Howe was waiting on the arrival of the British fleet to replenish his depleted stores. Only one thing stood between Howe and the approaching flotilla of 200 warships moving up the Delaware River—Fort Mifflin.

The fort was situated just south of Philadelphia on the Delaware River. A defensive bastion against any southern assault on the city, Fort Mifflin was besieged by ships of the British Empire, which had built it in 1772. For over seven weeks, the garrison in the fort held out against the massive fleet that was trying to push through the Delaware River. The heated artillery battle was abruptly concluded on November 10, when the British ships finally maneuvered into a decisive position around the fort.

Mifflin was consumed in a roaring blaze when the surrounding ships unleashed a devastating bombardment. It has been described as one of the most intense artillery barrages that has ever been launched in North America, in which roughly 1000 cannonballs crashed into the fort every 20 minutes. By the time the British ceased fire, the fort's walls had been leveled, the buildings inside had been flattened and nearly three-quarters of the garrison were dead or wounded.

Fort Mifflin was rebuilt in 1795, and it was manned by an active garrison during the War of 1812. Used as a prison camp during the Civil War, the fort lost much of its strategic value as the years passed, and was taken out of service in 1904.

Today, the fort is a national historical site situated between Philadelphia International Airport and the city's outer limits. The historical guides at Fort Mifflin dress in period costumes, hosting daily activities and reenactments for those interested in Pennsylvania's history. Over the years, however, many visitors have been treated to reenactments a bit too bizarre to be the work of human hands. And a number of staff members have come to realize that Fort Mifflin's history isn't restricted to the written page, but is constantly being brought back to life by a handful of spirits that haunt the place.

Not only the site of massive loss of life in 1777, the fort has also been host to a few other tragedies during its years of activity. Among the innumerable spirits of long-dead soldiers is the famous Screaming Lady whose remorseful wails are still heard from the old officer's quarters.

Although the details of Elizabeth Pratt's life have faded over the years, what remains certain is that she lived near Fort Mifflin and had a daughter who was involved with one of the fort's officers. When Mrs. Pratt learned of the illicit affair, she was so enraged that she disowned her only child. But irrepressible anger turned to heartrending regret when Elizabeth's daughter died of dysentery shortly

Many American patriots were killed when Fort Mifflin was bombarded by a devastating artillery attack in 1777.

afterward, in 1801. Unable to accept that her estranged child had passed away without her close by, Elizabeth committed suicide one year later.

The tortured soul of Elizabeth Pratt has remained behind in old Fort Mifflin. It is thought that the blood-curdling screams that echo through the night are the sounds of her guilt-ridden conscience, unable to expunge the demons that drove her to death. People who have heard the long, anguished wails of the Screaming Lady have never been able to forget them. On some occasions, her screams have been known to rise above the low-flying jets landing in the nearby airport. Once, passersby were so

Even when no historical reenactment is underway, the unmistakable clang of hammer against anvil echoes in the fort's smithy.

alarmed by the sound of the screaming coming from Mifflin that they thought a woman was being assaulted and called police. When investigators looked through the fort that night, they found nothing.

Not that the Screaming Lady has never been spotted. Although she remains hidden from adult eyes, groups of schoolchildren have inquired about the "gray lady" staring at them from the window of the old officer's quarters. Guides who look at the window see only an empty window frame. This same phenomenon has recurred too many times to ignore, causing some paranormal believers to wonder why the Screaming Lady appears before children and not adults. It could be that the Screaming Lady chooses to be seen only by the young because the attention of children eases the pain of her own earthly suffering. Or maybe children remind Elizabeth of her daughter before their relationship went sour. There's also the possibility that only children are capable of seeing her, their senses still able to perceive objects that adults have learned not to see.

Nevertheless, many adults have had no problems detecting the other spirits of Fort Mifflin. So many ghosts have been seen in the old fort that one might wonder if Mifflin isn't manned by a full ghostly garrison. Given the number of revolutionary soldiers who fell at their posts in the autumn of 1777, it wouldn't be surprising. Investigating psychics have already identified a number of the supernatural soldiers who, to this day, still carry out their final earthly duties.

One soldier who has continued to make his rounds in Mifflin used to be responsible for lighting the fort's oil lamps at twilight. Seen during the early evening hours, he is a faint transparent apparition holding a long stick with a faint light pulsating at the end. The figure is too faded to reveal details of the uniform or face, but a visiting medium sensed that this man's name was John. Almost always appearing on the second-floor balcony of the barracks, the image of the long-dead lamplighter drifts through the barracks before gradually dissipating into thin air.

He is not the only ghost in Fort Mifflin who seems to carry on his earthly duties into the afterlife. Many visitors have heard the metallic crash of hammer onto anvil resounding from the fort's restored smithy. They probably assumed that a historical reenactment was in progress. In actuality, the iron was cold, and no forging was taking place in the old blacksmith shop. What they had heard was the sound of one of the fort's deceased blacksmiths clattering around in his shop long past the normal hours of his workday. Visitors at the fort who interrupted what they were doing to take in the sight of an old smithy at work were invariably shocked to find an empty, suddenly silent chamber.

Various other spirits have been spotted at the fort. Some people claim to have seen the apparition of a bewildered revolutionary soldier wandering through the compound, checking his rifle, apparently waiting for an order that will never come. In the armory, there have been multiple sightings of an artillery captain who carefully oversees the fort's magazine.

But all who have conducted paranormal studies of Fort Mifflin agree that the most haunted area is the casemates that stretch under the walls facing the river. These big inhospitable rooms, located close to the original fort's main gates and the ruins of the walls that were obliterated over 200 years ago, seem to be packed full of ghosts.

Mediums who have identified several Revolutionary War ghosts suggest that these spirits might still be reeling from the violence of their demise. The terror they experienced during the bombardment was traumatic enough to create residual energy patterns—patterns manifested as

Ghosts of the Civil War, including the so-called Faceless Man, wander the corridors of the fort's eerie dungeon.

ghosts in the casemates. These spirits have appeared to people in a number of different ways. Some show as faint bluish lights glowing dimly in the darkness of the subterranean rooms. Others manifest as fearful men in 18th-century uniforms who stand next to the fireplace in one of the chambers.

Another group of apparitions spotted in the crowded casemates have their origins in the Civil War period. During the war, Fort Mifflin was used as a military prison, and the chambers under its walls were turned into holding cells for Confederate prisoners of war and Union deserters. The miseries these men endured appear to have lived on after the men died. According to paranormal investigators, visitors have felt sudden chills wash over them as they walked through Mifflin's underground halls or observed faint outlines of men sitting in the casemates. Some of these entities guard the entrances to the cells, while others—the Confederate captives—wait for the war to end. The most unfortunate of all are the Union deserters who wait feverishly for court-martial.

The story of the Faceless Man is the most familiar story from this period in the building's history. One of Mifflin's most visible ghosts, the Faceless Man was a Civil War criminal interred in the fort's dungeons. Known as William Howe when he was alive, the Union soldier was locked away for desertion and the murder of a superior officer. Legend has it that the black bag tied around his head before he was hanged was never removed when he was buried, and he returned to the casemates in Mifflin the same way he had been led out. The Faceless Man appears in the doorway of one of the cells, a faint apparition with a void where his face should be.

All the stories surrounding Mifflin might leave one with the impression that the fort is the Amityville of historic sites. In reality, most visitors will likely find themselves more intrigued by the fort's capable staff than spooked by its garrison of ghosts. Nevertheless, one cannot deny the huge number of stories that circulate about the place, making it one of the more prominent sites on Pennsylvania's paranormal map. It stands as yet another example of how history and the supernatural so often go hand in hand.

3
Haunted
Hospitality

~

For the most part, ghosts prefer to haunt private places. The extreme circumstances that are usually associated with lingering spirits are akin to the idiosyncrasies of individuals— in other words, haunts, like people, appear to be more comfortable finding expression behind closed doors, in the safety of their homes. But not always.

Some ghosts have no qualms with sharing their supernatural foibles with the general population. Unlike haunted houses, which affect a smaller number of people, these public hauntings are usually widely reported within the county they occur. Whether proprietors like it or not, their businesses and hotels often become associated with the ghosts that haunt them, and these buildings most readily become paranormal landmarks among enthusiasts. If the reader were to inquire about ghosts with a town local, these are the stories that would likely surface. Ask someone in Hollidaysburg about the U.S. Hotel, or an employee of Shawnee State Park about the Jean Bonnet Tavern. These tales are woven into the fabric of the place, passed on through generations of patrons and proprietors who call the stories their own.

~

Supernatural Terror in Hollidaysburg

The U.S. Hotel in Hollidaysburg was built in 1835, the same year that the Allegheny Portage Railroad reached town, linking it by railroad with the Pennsylvania Canal. Seeking to capitalize on the sudden east-west flow of people through Hollidaysburg, an entrepreneur named John Dougherty financed the construction of the hotel. He proceeded to ply weary 19th-century travelers with lodging, food and liquor. The hotel was Dougherty's cash cow until 1871, when a fire destroyed everything inside the three-story tavern.

A German immigrant named Engelbert Gromiller rebuilt the U.S. Hotel in 1886, also establishing a brewery next door. The hotel did business until the 1920s, when Prohibition made alcohol illegal. Used as a radio school and barracks for the United States Navy during the Second World War, the hotel changed hands a number of times after mid-century, slowly falling into disrepair. Renovations began on the old building in 1987, and something of the building's original opulence was restored on the ground floor. Today, the first floor of the U.S. Hotel is a fine restaurant run by Joe, Karen and Jason Yoder.

Such is what we might call the official history of the U.S. Hotel. However, it is those unrecorded events in the building's past—those shady episodes that earn the status of legend, rumor or bald-faced lie—that are of most concern to the people who operate the establishment today.

Could the second floor have really been a brothel, as some people say? Were there once tunnels under the U.S. Hotel that were used as a temporary stop for runaway slaves on the Underground Railroad? These questions are important because some things about the U.S. Hotel today just don't seem to jibe with the laws of science that govern the physical world. They are the kind of phenomena that, more often than not, make us turn our eyes to the past in search of supernatural explanations for the unnatural situations that some of us have been unfortunate enough to experience.

According to Patty Wilson's article in the October 2001 issue of *FATE* magazine, ("The Haunted U.S. Hotel: Anatomy of a Paranormal Investigation"), the first reports she heard about the strange events in the hotel were innocuous enough. The staff told some stories about the entity they named "Sarah," a mischievous spirit that knocked things off tables, opened the wine cabinet and generally made herself difficult any way she could. There was also the account of the worker who had slept in one of the rooms on the unfinished second floor after a day of renovations. The story goes that he woke up in the middle of the night to see a woman dressed in a white gown hovering about a foot and a half above the floor.

When Patty Wilson, Al Brindza and Scott Crown-over—the three core members of a Pennsylvanian ghost-hunting society called the Paranormal Research Foundation—got wind of the goings-on at the U.S. Hotel, they promptly organized an investigation. For those unfamiliar with the subculture of paranormal investigators that thrives across the nation, ghost-hunting societies are groups of people who dedicate much of their free time to searching for evidence of paranormal activity. Venturing into any area where ghosts are reported to be, ghost hunters attempt to capture hard evidence of the existence of supernatural phenomena with cameras, tape recorders, digital thermometers and electromagnetic field detectors. Although many ghost-hunting societies include psychics among their numbers, the primary aim of these groups is to obtain irrefutable objective evidence of supernatural activity.

Patty writes that it was on a night just before Thanksgiving when the Paranormal Research Foundation ventured into the U.S. Hotel. Scott, Patty and Al brought three other prospective ghost hunters with them on that cold November evening. Greeted by Karen Yoder, the ghost hunters waited at one of the tables until the last customers cleared out of the restaurant. Not until the group of six was alone with Karen did the investigation commence.

Ms Yoder's only strange experiences in the hotel involved the wine cabinet at the front entrance. Locking up the antique cabinet every evening before she left, she would find the cabinet door hanging wide open on more than one occasion when she opened it up the next morning. Many of the staff at the U.S. Hotel had similar experiences, disconcerting happenings that they blamed on a presence they called "Sarah."

But for the Paranormal Research Foundation, the most dramatic findings would be on the largely deserted second floor of the building. In her article for *FATE*, Patty Wilson states that what transpired there that evening was so powerful that it would forever change her relationships with Al and Scott.

It was about half past midnight when the investigators began their march up the creaky stairs to the big building's second floor. They split up into three groups of two, with each pair assigned to one of the three hallways that traversed that story. Wilson writes that two of the newcomers were sent to stake out the office, where in the past it was reported that the computer would turn off and on. It was the same room where the worker had awoken to the sight of the woman floating above the floor. Meanwhile, Scott and a college student named Stacie went through a big wooden door and down another hallway. This part of the building was pitch black and freezing cold, so the couple zipped up tight, turned on their flashlights and went ahead. It was Patty and Al's job to keep an overall watch of the floor, checking up on both parties to make sure that things were going fine.

But despite the pair's professionalism and experience, things would get pretty far from fine before very long. It all started with a loud scream from the same hall that Scott and Stacie had walked down. Patty and Al swung open the door that opened onto the hallway to see the young woman running toward them with a look of complete fear in her eyes. She was terrified, crying "I've got to get out of here!" over and over in a desperate mantra of fear.

Scott was right behind her, trying to calm her down as they rushed by Al and Patty. At one point Scott tried to physically stop her, but Stacie, propelled by her fear, was dragging her partner along with her.

Scott Crownover managed to stop long enough to give his colleagues a quick explanation, but there wasn't much to his story. He told Al and Patty about a bedroom door at the end of the hallway. The only warning he got that Stacie was about to act unusually came seconds after he opened the door. She was murmuring something about the room being creepy one moment, and then she was running down the hall the next, yelling repeatedly, "I've got to get out of here!"

After Scott finished telling Patty and Al what had happened, he continued after Stacie, who had disappeared down the stairs. Patty and Al were left standing in sudden silence. They stood at the door, peering into the darkness of the hallway. "Well," Patty said, breaking the silence, "I guess we better see what happened." Al Brindza nodded his head in stoic agreement.

They slowly made their way down the cold hallway, stopping at the door Stacie had fled from. A large bed was barely visible in the darkness within. Hoping to capture something on camera that might be invisible to the naked eye, Al tried to snap a picture, but his camera was jammed. Ghost hunters have learned from experience that malfunctioning electronic equipment is often a sign of a supernatural presence. Patty grabbed her own camera and took a picture.

In the blue-lit instant of Patty's camera flash, a woman appeared lying on the bed. She was young with tangled chestnut hair. Clutching her head in her hands, her face was frozen in an aspect of extreme pain, her legs curled under a brown blanket. The image lasted only for the duration of the flash, but it left an indelible imprint in

Patty's mind. This ghost was the first one that she had ever seen firsthand.

She turned her back to the scene, looking out the window, trying hard to maintain her composure. Al could see her face in the half-light of the window, and he knew then that what he had seen by the camera's flash wasn't a figment of his imagination. "You saw her, too," he said. Patty didn't have to respond to her colleague; he could see the answer in her eyes.

As Patty would later recount, the sighting had been a traumatic experience, and the two ghost hunters spent the next few moments pulling themselves together, steeling themselves for whatever was to come. Yet when they shone a flashlight into the dark room, there was no one there. A large wood-framed bed stood against the far wall, but that was it; the flashlight revealed no tortured woman writhing under the blankets. The room was empty.

Or at least it looked empty in the dim stream of light emitted by their flashlight. The moment Patty and Al stepped into the room, however, they knew that there was more there than met the eye. The air in the bedroom, even colder than the frigid hallway, crackled with an invisible energy. Without saying a word to each other, Patty and Al instinctually concentrated on the door in the opposite wall, moving through the strange bedroom as quickly as they could. Little did they know that the worst was yet to come.

Making their way through the doorway at the other end of the room, Pat and Al found themselves in another hallway. Standing just outside the room, the two were suddenly barely able to breathe, as if some invisible blanket was smothering them both. It was at that moment that a large black shadow formed from the darkness on one of the hallway walls, a shadow with a life of its own. The dark silhouette detached itself from the wall and darted down the dark hallway before them. Acting purely on what can only be described as ghost hunters' instincts, the two ran after the black shape.

The suffocating feeling ended the moment they moved away from the door. The weight in their lungs was replaced by the booming of their fear-stricken hearts as they sprinted through the darkness after the unknown shape. Their chase led them to an empty room strewn with garbage. The only way onward was through a door on the opposite wall, which they soon found led down to the building's old office. Just through the door was where the chase ended with Al stopping suddenly. "He's down there," he whispered to Patty through tight breath, pausing before he added, "I can't go down."

The air began to grow heavy on them again, and once more it was getting hard to breathe, as if the very atmosphere was conspiring to suffocate them. That was when they heard Scott's voice. He was back at the haunted bedroom, heading toward them with an emboldened Stacie right behind. Patty and Al headed back toward the bedroom, meeting Scott and Stacie halfway down the hall.

By now there was ample evidence that something was very wrong in the hotel. And whereas Patty, Stacie and Al had all witnessed some of the traumatic happenings on the second floor, Scott was still raring to go. He argued that the group should take a look at the third level, and they agreed with varying degrees of enthusiasm. Patty, Scott and Stacie would make the ascent to the third floor. Meanwhile, saying that he wanted to take a closer look around, Al Brindza, the foundation's premier psychic, planned to remain behind at the doorway to the bedroom where the dark-haired woman had been seen.

Leaving Al behind on the darkened second floor, Scott led Patty and Stacie to the wooden stairs that gave access to the third floor. The hesitant trio was about halfway up the stairs when a booming voice from down below stopped them where they stood. It was Al's voice, but tinged with such a level of terrible urgency that it was almost unrecognizable, bearing no trace of the soft-spoken man's normally gentleness. "Patty!" Al roared from the darkness below, "Get them down now!"

Stacie led the charge back down the stairs, almost falling over herself in her rush to get back to the ground floor. At the main stairs, the trio ran into Al, who said nothing to Patty or Scott but just followed Stacie down to the first floor, doing everything he could to remain composed. It was a thin veneer of calmness, however, and it was clear from his stilted stride and the panic in his eyes that Al was in a deep state of shock.

Mike and Janelle, the two novice ghost hunters who had remained in the computer room, were relieved from their lookout, and the entire expedition retired to the restaurant. Stacie was sitting at a table, deathly still, white as a ghost and staring blankly ahead. Whatever she had experienced on the second floor was still wreaking havoc on her mind. The investigation was definitely more than she had bargained for.

As for Al, the veteran ghost hunter was alone in the bathroom, painfully clutching his stomach and leaning heavily against a wall, not even bothering to look up when Scott entered. Scott asked his friend if he was all right, but Al could only dismiss him with a weak wave of his hand, too drained even to speak. Meanwhile, Stacie began to speak about her own encounter on the second floor. It turned out that she had suddenly been filled with a feeling of absolute dread, as if her very life was in imminent danger.

Al eventually stumbled out of the bathroom, telling everyone that he was OK. His shouted warning, he said, had been a result of a feeling similar to Stacie's— a strong sense that they should all leave while they could. Later that night, when Al was sure he was alone with Patty and Scott, he revealed the true nature of what he has seen.

"Upstairs, when I told you to get down," Al explained, as related by Patty in her *FATE* article, "I was looking through that room when a shadow stepped into the light. He was carrying an axe or something. I knew just then that he had killed that girl on the bed. He had hacked her to death." As Al spoke of what he had experienced, his face began to pale, and he soon regained the terrified aspect he had been wearing in the bathroom. He looked as though he had witnessed this young woman's murder firsthand.

Although Stacie and Al were anxious to leave after everything that had occurred around the second floor bedroom, Patty wanted to take one more look. "I can't stand a bully," Patty would later explain. "Somehow that male shadow seemed like a bully to me, and despite feeling unnerved, I needed to go back and prove that I would not let him frighten me away."

Accompanied by Scott and Mike, Patty made one more foray to the bedroom on the second floor. She was about to get a taste of what Al experienced earlier. The moment Patty walked into the haunted bedroom, her mind was possessed by two fierce telepathic voices. "Run!" a woman's voice seemed to scream into her ear. "Get out of here!"

The woman's desperate pleas were answered by a rough male voice roaring in psychopathic rage. She couldn't make out much of what he was saying, but Patty heard the word "bitch" numerous times, and she felt that she had become the focus of an immense hatred. For a woman to remain in the same room that this rabidly misogynous man had occupied, even though a century ago, would be to expose herself to a very real danger. Patty felt herself begin to swoon under the fierce barrage of hatred and had to lean on some stacked boxes to catch her breath.

The trio left the area. No one had any more desire to flirt with the supernatural that evening, so the Paranormal Research Foundation called it a night.

However, the investigators would not be able to leave the ghosts of the U.S. Hotel behind completely. Stacie had a horrible night's sleep that night, her rest racked by a series of horrific nightmares. The last dream was so bad that she got up and woke her boyfriend, hoping that a little conversation might help to ease her mind. Getting up to turn on the bedroom light, she screamed loudly when a dark shadow dashed across the room and disappeared. Her boyfriend had seen it too.

Meanwhile, Al was suffering through a torturous night as well. Struggling to fall asleep through fierce fits of nausea, he was promptly awakened by vivid nightmares whenever he managed to nod off. Every time he was startled awake, he would hear harsh whispering in the dark and see a dark shadow move quickly away from his bed.

It seems that whatever malevolent force haunts the U.S. Hotel has no qualms about following visitors home. The rub is that no one is really sure what that persistent presence on the second floor is. Certainly there is nothing about the building's history that suggests anything unusual. Rumors have circulated that there once was a brothel on the second floor. Other stories describe tunnels underneath the building that were used before the Civil War as temporary housing for runaway slaves. But these are unofficial accounts, belonging more in the realm of legend than historical fact. What is clear to the paranormal investigators who have ventured up to the second floor is that something definitely happened there at one time—some appalling atrocity that the investigators would prefer not to talk about in detail.

Unless more about the U.S. Hotel's past comes to light, the strange goings-on in the building will remain of interest only to paranormal investigators and others who have had bizarre experiences in the building, rather than to people with a more strictly historical perspective. However, given the nature of those experiences, perhaps it is best that the events on the second floor remain buried in the building's history.

Ghosts of the Jean Bonnet Tavern

The Jean Bonnet was built to last. An impressive two-story stone structure constructed in the 1760s atop the foundations of a small French fort, the tavern has done almost 250 years of business in Bedford County. It is located three miles west of Bedford on Route 30, near Shawnee State Park, and today it operates as a bed and breakfast, providing fine food and comfortable accommodation to fortunate sightseers traveling that scenic stretch of highway through the Allegheny Mountains.

Boasting an authentic colonial character, with stone walls, chestnut beams and massive period fireplaces, the Jean Bonnet leaves most visitors to walk away impressed by its quaint bucolic charm. Underneath the tavern's enchanting ambience, however, lies a deep and dark history. The tavern has been a receptacle for no small amount of human misery in the two and a half centuries it has been open. The mix of history and local legend that is the tale of the Jean Bonnet Tavern is a story of death and heartache, telling of a time when the building served as a courthouse and prison. Here, accused men met their demise at the end of a hangman's noose, dangling from the same beams that are so prized for their aesthetic value today. These accounts may not rival the horrors of such famous historical penitentiaries as the Tower of London, but they are bloody enough for any humble 18th-century structure built on the frontier in western Pennsylvania. Given all the strange goings-on that afflict the tavern today, it seems as if the blood spilled there has not been completely washed away by the passage of years.

The first man reported to have died in the Jean Bonnet was a victim of military justice during the hard times of the French and Indian War. The year was 1758, and General John Forbes was billeted in the tavern for a short while during his march to the French-held Fort Duquesne on the Ohio River. It was still months before the battle that would have Duquesne renamed Pittsburgh, and the general had stopped at the tavern to consider his course through the Alleghenies. He was studying maps and receiving intelligence reports in the Jean Bonnet's main room when it was brought to his attention that a certain man staying in the tavern was showing a little too much interest in Forbes' orders to his subordinates.

The man brought before the general turned out to be a local teamster, and after he was subjected to the thumb-screws of military interrogation, he confessed to being a spy for the French. Later on that day, the fatally curious teamster was hanged in the tavern, left dangling there as Forbes and his men resumed their march west.

It would not be the last time the Jean Bonnet Tavern was used to carry out corporal punishment. The region lacked a formal courthouse for much of the following century, and the local settlers took to using the second floor of the tavern as an impromptu courtroom when the occasion called. Documented evidence shows that at least seven people were sentenced to death and hanged on the second floor, their remains being buried on the surrounding grounds.

The deaths that occurred in the Jean Bonnet were not just limited to harsh executions of justice as interpreted by early Pennsylvanians. One tale recounts a woman succumbing to an end that was gentler, if no less cruel. History has forgotten her name, but her passion for her beau was so fierce that it arguably lives on today. As is usually the case with stories of ghostly lovers, the affair between the two paramours was doomed to tragedy. Her love was the proprietor of the Jean Bonnet at that time. He was a wealthy businessman whose political convictions cast him on the side of the colonials when the American Revolution broke out, and he served as a scout for George Washington. A married man, he knew from the onset that nothing good could come from his rash affection for the pretty young woman who had become infatuated with him. But the Pennsylvanian belle, still burdened with the naiveté of youth, was convinced that things would work out for them. Although the innkeeper let his mistress stay in one of tavern rooms, between his duties for the Revolutionary Army and his marital obligations, months would go by with the lonely woman at the tavern not receiving even a word from him.

Employees at the tavern grew used to the sound of her footsteps dashing from her second floor bedroom whenever wagon or horse approached the Jean Bonnet. They would hear the woman run down the hall to the window, where she would look in vain for her coming lover. Disappointed almost every time, she slowly made a path back to her room, where she would remain for the rest of the day, until the sounds of approaching riders were heard again, whereupon she would dash down the hall to the window yet again. Days turned into weeks, which turned into months, and the constant disappointments

Corporal punishment and lost love contribute to the hauntings at the Jean Bonnet Tavern near Bedford.

of the ritualistic rushes to the second-floor window took a heavy toll on the woman's health. She died shortly after becoming bedridden with some unknown illness.

If such intense suffering is only another facet of existence, classified together with experiences of love and lumped together with boredom, past events at the Jean Bonnet Tavern would remain on the pages of those who document local histories. But as is so often the case with tragedies of this sort, they somehow find a way to leave an imprint on the space they occurred in. Even today, people at the Jean Bonnet Tavern find themselves having experiences that can't be explained by any rational means.

For instance, many different people have heard the sound of footsteps rushing from one of the second-floor rooms, down the hallway and to the window. The footsteps stop there for a few moments before slowly making their way back to the room they came from. Individuals who have been in that hallway when the footsteps moved between the room and the window have reported hearing the sound of rustling material as the invisible entity rushed by them, as if the ghost was a woman in a dress. As well, many of these people claim that a scent of rose perfume wafted by when the footsteps moved past. The predominant theory is that the spirit is that of the woman who died at the Jean Bonnet while she was waiting for her beau during the Revolutionary War, repeating the lonely trip from her room to the window and back again for a miserable eternity, day and night.

Men dressed in the rough frontier garb of early American settlers have often been spotted silently drifting through the halls of the Jean Bonnet, their expressions blank and transparent, moving toward the area that used to serve as a courthouse during centuries past. It was a room where men were tried by dubious methods and then hanged from any point from which a noose could be lashed. Other male apparitions have been spotted well after the sun has gone down, sitting blankly at a restaurant table on the ground floor.

Paranormal investigator and writer Patty Wilson tells of one bartender's experience with the ghost of what was presumably a convict: "This bartender was closing the place up one night not so long ago. It was getting near closing time, and the only other people there were the bartender's boyfriend and one patron that had obviously had a little too much to drink. The woman decided it would be best to put off her closing duties to drive the lone customer home and return later with her boyfriend to close up afterwards," Patty explains. The sight that greeted the bartender and her boyfriend when they returned to the Jean Bonnet that evening turned both of them into believers in the supernatural.

Patty Wilson continues: "The bartender was walking along the patio to the entrance of the tavern when, looking through the window, she saw a single man sitting at the bar by himself. Her first thought was that she had not noticed the man sitting there when she'd left, and locked him in."

The bartender rushed to the door and unlocked it, hoping that the man wouldn't be too angry at being locked in, but by the time she swung the door open she realized that she was apologizing to empty air: the man was nowhere to be found. Standing there in horror at the impossibility of the event that had just occurred, she looked over to her boyfriend, but it was instantly obvious by the look on his face that he had seen the same thing. Although she continued on as an employee at the Jean Bonnet, after that night she refused to ever close the bar again.

Another employee who experienced a disconcerting event in the Jean Bonnet was initially convinced that she was dealing only with a troublesome child, but she was to walk away from the encounter with an uneasy feeling in the pit of her stomach. It seemed innocent enough at first: a small family having supper in the restaurant with a child who was fixated on having some ice cream. The waitress and parents managed to convince the boy that he would get some ice cream after he was finished his dinner.

When it was finally time for dessert, the waitress, smiling widely, crouched to face level with the child and asked him what flavor he would like. The boy's shrill reaction startled everyone at the table, almost knocking the waitress off her feet. He began screaming uncontrollably, hollering "I wanna go now" over and over at the top of his lungs.

The parents, never having seen their child act this way, apologized, quickly paid their bill and started out the door, giving the waitress only one opportunity to ask the boy what was wrong. Between hysterical sobs, he barely managed to get out his response before his mother carried him out, "There were eyes in the wall," he wailed, "and they were watching me." Although the waitress would have liked to chalk up the kid's reaction to childish imagination, the all-too-real fear in the boy's eyes precluded any such explanation. Her eyes moved from the horror-struck boy to the wall he had recoiled from. She knew at that moment that the child was telling the truth; the look in the boy's eyes said it all—something supernatural had appeared in the restaurant wall.

Another account documents the stay of a military officer and his wife in the tavern. Woken in the middle of the night by the sound of the shower running, the man did not get up. He assumed that his wife was in the bathroom but wondered groggily why she was taking a shower at such a late hour. When he asked her about it the next morning, he was surprised to find that she had been awakened by the running water as well and was about ask him the same question.

Another story has a couple walking through the building, stretching their legs after a long day on the highway.

The door to their room was locked, and the couple's child was lying in their bed while his bottle of milk was cooling on the balcony. Neither the mother nor father thought it strange when their infant began to cry. He had been cranky for the last few hours in the car, hungry and restless in the confines of the automobile. Both parents' ears perked up, however, when their child's crying suddenly stopped. Unlocking the door, they were greeted with a sight that neither of them could explain. Their baby was lying contentedly on his back, sucking enthusiastically at the bottle in his mouth. Not only had the doors to the hallway and balcony been locked, but even if the baby could walk, there was no way he could have reached the bottle at the top of the railing. The first thing the child's mother did was ask the chambermaid if she had given the baby his bottle, but the woman hadn't even been on the same floor at the time.

Some supernatural phenomena occur on such a regular basis that they've almost come to be expected among patrons and employees at the Jean Bonnet. The most common such event occurs during the hours of darkness. Numerous guests have woken in the middle of the night to hear the sounds of bustling activity coming from the bar on the first floor. Many people that have been awakened by these sounds have lodged complaints with the management, arguing that the bar shouldn't be open when guests at the bed and breakfast are trying to sleep. Of course, these complaints have usually left the Jean Bonnet staff perplexed, because the bar is rarely, if ever, open late.

Patty Wilson recalls one man's experience with the ghosts in the bar. It was during the fall of 2000, and the man was one part of a three-man hunting trip that included his best friend and his 15-year-old son. Stirred out of his slumber by a racket from the bar below, the man was seized by a sudden late-night craving for orange juice. As the bar was obviously open, he decided to go downstairs to get some. We can only imagine his surprise when he made it down to the bar's entranceway only to find a dark empty room shut off by a barred and locked door.

"I swear to God I heard bar noises," the man told Patty, "glasses clanking, music, people talking. I wasn't the only one who heard it either; both my son and my buddy had heard the noises as well. I was convinced that someone was playing a joke on me, and ran over to the window...just to see how many cars were in the parking lot. There were none there but mine."

The story of the Jean Bonnet doesn't end there. Patty Wilson's Paranormal Research Foundation celebrated Christmas 2001 with an investigation of the Jean Bonnet. Given the history of the building, the investigators were not at all surprised by their findings. The Foundation's oddest discovery in the Jean Bonnet involved dramatic jumps in the readings of one of the investigators' EMF (electromagnetic field) meters, a tool used by ghost hunters to indicate the presence of spirits in an area. The strange thing about the EMF meter's readings was that the jumps in the meter's readings formed the rough outline of a human body lying on the ground, not unlike a police trace at the scene of a murder.

The investigator got her husband, a skeptic, to lie down in the position of the unusual readings. Sure enough, he fit into the area bounded by the high EMF readings; the EMF jump etched an almost perfect outline of a human body.

When a photograph taken of the investigator's husband lying on the tavern floor was developed, a glowing circle of light was seen hovering over his midsection— another one of the Jean Bonnet's ghosts. The tavern has become one of the Paranormal Research Foundation's premier investigation sites. Patty Wilson has written about it in her book, *Haunted Pennsylvania,* and she herself has investigated the building twice. No doubt there are plenty of ghosts to study in the impressive old colonial building.

The Tamaqua Elks Club

The small town of Tamaqua lies on U.S. 209, near the northeastern border of Schuylkill County. Once a center for the booming anthracite industry that dominated the region, Tamaqua has since settled into peaceful repose— just another small Pennsylvania town tucked away in the verdant countryside. This is not to say that Tamaqua has faded into anonymity. One of the town's buildings has attracted the attention of a good number of paranormal enthusiasts, bringing people from all across the state to the doorstep of the local Elks Club building, seeking access to the old structure's famous third floor.

Built in the 1800s, this stone edifice is one of Tamaqua's oldest standing buildings. Purchased by the Elks Club in 1906, it has served as a tavern, restaurant and meeting area for the local Elks. With a bar on the first floor, a dining room and meeting hall on the second, and boarding rooms and a ballroom on the third, there was more than enough business coming in to keep the Elks' building afloat. Today, however, the only people who venture up to the top floor of the building are reluctant Elks employees whose work duties take them there—or paranormal investigators actively seeking some kind of encounter with the denizens of the afterworld. Seldom do those who journey to Tamaqua for this purpose leave the building disappointed.

Following the Elks' 1906 acquisition of the structure, decades passed with nothing out of the ordinary occurring within its walls. Then, early one morning years ago, some early risers found one of the boarders hanging by her neck from the staircase banister on the third floor. All evidence led to the conclusion that the woman had taken her own life. Although no one knows for certain what drove her to do such a horrible thing, subsequent events suggested that it may have been a family issue, for, a few years later, this woman's brother decided on a disturbingly similar course of action. Checking into the Elks Club for an evening, he was found the next morning dangling at the end of rope tied to his doorframe.

Two suicides taking place in the same building was enough to get people talking, but when it became general knowledge that the pair were brother and sister, people began attaching bizarre stories to the third floor. It was at this time that people's accounts of eerie experiences on the top floor started to appear in the local canon of urban legend. Everyone knew someone who knew somebody who had heard footsteps in the hallway when there was no one there. Others spoke of doors slamming shut or opening in the absence of any visible physical force. There were also reports of inexplicable cold spells; a comfortable room would become like a meat locker within a short few minutes, only to gradually warm up again, all for no discernable reason.

The tenor of these stories changed after 1970, when another person was found dead in one of the boarding rooms. Although this man died of natural causes, probably expiring peacefully while in his sleep, things on the third floor took a marked turn shortly after his passing. Whereas earlier stories about the Elks Club's top floor were tinged with the whimsy of any tall tale, guests' accounts grew evermore frequent and darker after this last man's passing on. A very real fear of the boarding rooms took root among the visitors to the Elks Club, and business on the third floor began to suffer.

One man walking to his room late in the evening was confronted by what he would later describe as a humanoid shadow, a black featureless shape moving down the hall toward him. The man could only stand speechless as the figure passed right through his body, leaving him shivering in cold and unable to breath as it continued past. The experience was so traumatic that he packed up his things and left that night, never to return. Another boarder spent an entire evening lying fearfully in bed, fixated on a dark corner in his room. He could see nothing there, but he could swear that some sort of malevolent presence was silently looming there, staring at him with an ineffable hatred. Too scared to fall asleep, too scared to move, the man left the Elks Club at first light, and he never went up to the third floor again.

People spoke of the new chill that permeated the air on the third floor, of a strange kind of heaviness that hung in the ether, blanketing all light in a thin filter, deepening shadows and smothering light. The previously fanciful tales about the building were being transformed into terrifying personal experiences.

Stories of these experiences circulated through Tamaqua and beyond, branding the Elks Club meeting hall as one of the county's haunted sites. The number of boarders shrank so much that it was no longer feasible to keep the third floor open, and the rooms were closed to the public early in the 1970s.

Since then, most people have tended to stay away from the third story. Although the bar and restaurant on the first and second floors still attract patrons, very few people now venture up to the now infamous top floor. But the experiences of those who have climbed the building's last flight of stairs have been more than enough to keep the Elks Club's supernatural reputation alive and well.

For example, there is the story of the lone plumber who was working in one of the third-floor rooms. He was inspecting a pipe that ran behind the walls when the door to the room violently slammed shut behind him. Puzzled and a little startled, the man walked across the room to open the door, only to discover that it had been locked. More angry than he was frightened, the plumber began banging on the door, yelling at whoever had locked him in to let him out. About 10 minutes went by before he heard the latch click open. A loud rebuke was already halfway past his lips as he swung the door open, but he cut himself off when he stepped into the darkened, completely deserted hallway; there was no one there. Realizing that there was no way anyone could have fled down the hallway that quickly, the man turned back to his work, finishing up in the suddenly foreboding room as quickly as he could before bolting back down to the main floor. Here was another man who promised himself never to venture up the Elks Club's stairs again.

More than one paranormal investigator has visited Tamaqua in hopes of seeing one of the Elks Club's ghosts. For several years now, the spirits of the third floor have come under the scrutiny of a multitude of psychics and ghost hunters. Their findings have done nothing but substantiate the local stories about the building.

Almost every kind of supernatural indicator that paranormal investigators are able to detect has been recorded in the Elks building at one time or another. Glowing circles of light have turned up in droves in photographs taken on the Elks Club third floor. Referred to as "orbs" by ghost hunters, they are thought to indicate ghosts. In addition to photographs riddled with inexplicable pinpoints of light, ghost hunters have recorded completely unaccountable drops in temperature. There have been occasions when psychics have been grabbed by ice-cold hands that seem to have come out of the very walls. Others have had terrifying visions of figures cloaked in flame roaring at them to get off the third floor. These experiences have been recorded by different paranormal societies, adding to the substantial store of local accounts regarding the third floor.

A ghost hunter named Sean Snyder has done some of his own research on the third floor, adding his experiences there to the ever-growing body of supernatural accounts in the Elks Club building. Arriving in Tamaqua early in November 2001, the young ghost enthusiast set up for what was to be one of his most dramatic investigations.

Snyder began with photographs of the enigmatic bloodstain located beneath the banister of the third-floor stairs, just under the area where the woman hanged herself so many years ago. The owners have painted over the reddish-brown mark several times, but no matter how thick the coat, the stain continues to reappear, a reminder of one woman's miserable demise at the end of a rope.

"There really was a lot of supernatural activity there," Snyder recalled the following year. "We took 22 pictures with orbs in them." The shots were taken whenever the photographer felt anything out of the ordinary. If he was struck by sudden chills while standing in a room, Snyder would point and click at the air around him. Most of these photos yielded orbs hovering all around, invisible to the naked eye, but somehow registering on celluloid.

"My father arrived near the end of the investigation," Snyder recalls. "He was standing in one of the rooms when he was hit by this weird sensation that the ground was going beneath him." When Sean's father told him what he was feeling, the ghost investigator snapped a shot of his dad. Sure enough, the photograph revealed the presence of a large orb hovering just above Mr. Snyder's head.

Sean's findings were not limited to stationary orbs in still photographs. He also caught six moving orbs on video camera. These entities, invisible to the naked eye as well, appear on video as streaking balls of light, moving quickly across the picture.

No single theory convincingly explains what these moving lights are, but some investigators have dramatic footage showing what happened when orbs have collided with the people filming them. And though these orbs are not seen without the aid of a video camera, they are definitely felt, for people have been jarred, startled, or profoundly terrified when they felt the sudden impact of a moving orb.

In one particular corner of a certain third-floor room, previous investigators have often had fairly intense supernatural experiences. Some groups have been suddenly seized by the undeniable feeling that someone or something was standing right beside them. It was here that one psychic felt a frigid hand come through the wall and grab her, and it was here that the terrifying flaming figure has appeared to sensitive mediums, demanding they leave the room immediately. Snyder was standing in this room when the temperature suddenly plummeted and all of his recording equipment cut out on him. There was no reasonable explanation. Not even a trace of a draft whispered through the room, and all the batteries in his equipment were fresh. "It only lasted for a couple of seconds," Sean remembers, "and then the temperature went back to normal, and all the equipment just turned on again."

There one moment, gone the next—whatever force was acting in that corner left no kind of explanation for its visitation, leaving Sean wondering what had just happened, and why. The erratic jumps of his EMF (electromagnetic field) meter did not help at all. Although it was obvious that something was disrupting the electromagnetic field on the third floor, he could only hazard guesses at what kind of force it might be.

His investigation completed, Sean Snyder filed his notes with those relating to all his other explorations in eastern Pennsylvania. His reports, like those of many paranormal societies across the country, are well stocked with empirical observation but show a rather conspicuous shortage of sound explanations. The suicides that took place on the third floor in the Elks Club building, for example, seem to have something to do with the bizarre goings-on there, but there is no way of knowing how or why these spirits remain behind. Although neither Sean Snyder nor any other ghost hunter can claim to have the definitive explanation, it may be said that nothing less than the mysteries of the afterlife are locked within such hauntings as those in the Tamaqua building. And as long as questions of life, death, and the soul remain mysteries to humanity, the proprietors of the Elks Club can continue to expect visitors interested in looking through their third floor.

The Murders at the Blue Ball Inn

Had she been judged by her outward appearance alone, Priscilla Moore Robinson could only have been suspected of compulsive cleanliness. With her starched white bonnet and the well-ironed pleats in her perennially bleached apron, the proprietor of the Blue Ball Inn was about as sanitized as people of the 18th century could be. Yet there was more to "Old Prissy" than a scrubbed and pressed wardrobe. Some patrons caught her staring at certain individuals when she thought no one was looking. Her cold eyes gleamed with a sudden and fierce malevolence while the deep lines in her face bent into creases of hatred. Anyone who saw Priscilla in this light was never able to look at her in any other way ever again. The sturdy matriarch of the Chester County inn was transformed into someone who, at that moment, was capable of anything.

We may never know the inner workings of Old Prissy's mind, but it seems that some part of her depravity may have been a reaction to the instability of her times. Born in 1760, Priscilla witnessed huge changes during her 100 years: the United States emerged from the 13 original colonies, the steam-driven train replaced the horse-drawn wagon and the Industrial Revolution, which she did not understand, practically remade the world she lived in. Such momentous developments would be hard for any person to digest in one lifetime, but to a person like Priscilla, whose naturally suspicious character was spiced with generous doses of red-hot rancor, the temper of the times fostered a deeply ingrained misanthropy.

Priscilla's grandfather, Dr. Bernhard van Leer, purchased the Blue Ball Inn and the 209 acres it was situated on in 1759. The inn was located on the well-traveled Old Lancaster Road and made a good business off travelers between Philadelphia and Lancaster. In 1794, however, a new stone turnpike was constructed a few miles north of the Blue Ball, isolating the tavern from the steady east-west flow of traffic. Priscilla was 34 years old when the new turnpike jeopardized the family business. Despite all the hard work that she had put into the tavern, she learned that her own livelihood largely depended on forces beyond her control.

The owner of the now-deserted inn responded by building another Blue Ball Inn, this one much larger than the first establishment. Constructed from Pennsylvania trapstone and fitted with odd crescent-shaped windows cut into the rooms on the third floor, the inn was built right next to the new stone turnpike. Shortly after the relocation, Priscilla took over the proprietorship of the inn, and it was then that people in the area began to talk, with fearful glances and hurried whispers, about the unnerving goings-on at the Blue Ball Inn.

Something ugly had overtaken Priscilla Robinson by the time she was in her mid-30s. Her sudden fits of hatred for the people around her—which had already occurred periodically when she was younger—came more frequently. Her face assumed a permanent mask of mild loathing, and the cold glint in her dark eyes shone like a full moon in January. Any person glancing at her would have easily believed any one of the stories about the mad innkeeper in Daylesford that were circulating around Chester County.

Not only did Priscilla's first husband, Edward Robinson, vanish mysteriously shortly after the new inn was opened, but there were accounts of more than one visitor disappearing in the middle of the night. The first time it happened, some patrons were awakened from sleep in the early hours with the sounds of several muffled thuds. A few minutes later, they heard another sound—a slow, grating noise coming from the kitchen downstairs, as if someone down below was digging a shovel into hard, dry dirt.

The next morning, guests in the common room muttered among themselves. Those who had heard the noises during the night were already suspicious, and it was only a matter of time before someone pointed out that one of the patrons was missing.

Old Prissy eventually emerged from the kitchen, laden with trays of hot breakfast and strong coffee, her heavily starched clothing practically crackling as she buzzed around the customers. Nothing in her demeanor betrayed any sense of guilt, and she casually disregarded any questions about the missing patron.

"Bah," the stocky innkeeper exclaimed, "serves the drunk lout right, rummaging through my bar for free whiskey." Old Prissy swept the room with her fierce gaze and a thick silence fell over the lot. She let the silence linger for a few seconds before concluding, "So I threw the thief out into the night." And that would be the end of the issue.

Over the years, this scene repeated itself on a number of different occasions, and the Blue Ball Inn slowly acquired a reputation for mysteriously swallowing up guests. Old Prissy aged into a fierce old woman, staunchly dedicated to keeping her tavern spotless, a task she was more successful at than she was at keeping her name clean. One woman who spent the night at the tavern was found the next morning hanging over the stairs to the second floor, strung up by the neck. Priscilla was unconcerned, stating that she had no idea why the woman would want to commit suicide in her inn. Few believed that the death was self-inflicted. Along with all the bizarre events, Priscilla went through two more husbands after her first marriage. Both John Cahill and John Fisher disappeared without a trace soon after marrying, and their bodies were never found. Somehow, locals were not bothered that Old Prissy was the only thrice-widowed woman in Chester County.

Most of Priscilla's later years were spent battling the railroad. Because she had lived to see the construction of a turnpike make the first Blue Ball Inn obsolete, she probably wasn't surprised when the railroad linking Philadelphia to Lancaster was completed, rendering her roadside inn—and the road it was situated on—largely unnecessary. Not surprised, but not happy either. Old Prissy made it a habit to go out and meet the train, yelling profanities at the iron horse as it passed by. The sight of the curmudgeonly old lady hobbling after the train, cursing with a sailor's vocabulary, struck the engineers as hilarious, and they began having fun with her. When she appeared next to the track, they blew the train's whistle and waved to her happily in mock greeting. This only infuriated her more. To add insult to injury, the train station in nearby Paoli caused business to boom for her prime competitor, the General Paoli Inn.

Things came to a head when the train ran over a cow of Old Prissy's that had been grazing near the tracks. When her demands for reparation were not immediately met, she took matters into her own hands. Smearing the tracks with fat from her dead cow, she stood by and watched gleefully as the train approached the slick rails. Its wheels spun ineffectually when it hit the slippery metal, unable to make it up the gradual incline into Paoli. It slowly slid to a complete stop. Thrilled that she had gotten the train to stop, Old Prissy broke into a jig in front of the outraged engineers and delivered insults between fits of sardonic laughter. She was reimbursed for her dead cow that same day.

Priscilla had become something of a folk hero, the lone individual taking a stand against the big money of the railroads. But she was a folk hero with a failing business, a dark past and a difficult disposition. When Old Prissy passed away in 1860, she quickly faded into anonymity.

No one could get comfortable in the Blue Ball Inn after Prissy died. Anybody who spent any time in the building became convinced that it was haunted. Odd noises were heard coming from the ground-floor kitchen, and sudden screams in the middle of the night were an all-too-frequent occurrence. The Blue Ball couldn't attract any employees, let alone customers, and in 1894 it was sold to new owners who were intent on converting the inn into a home. During the ensuing renovations, the rumors of atrocity in the Blue Ball Inn from so many years earlier were finally corroborated by hard material evidence.

Six skeletons were dug up in the kitchen cellar—the same kitchen that guests had heard the scraping sound come from years ago. Their split skulls made it obvious that they had died from fierce blows to the head. Another skeleton was found buried in the orchard with the same cleft in the skull. If Old Prissy was indeed the one who had murdered these victims, she was consistent in her method.

Accounts of haunted activity were reported soon after Priscilla's death, but following the disinterment of skeletal remains from the Blue Ball, the frequency of supernatural phenomena rose to new heights. The new residents claimed they saw the apparition of an old woman clothed in a blood-splattered dress walking through their house late in the evening. On other nights, the sounds of drawers violently opening and shutting were heard in the same room that Old Prissy had slept in when she was alive. Theories suggest that the unearthing of the skeletons had somehow recalled the emotional trauma of the murders, and that the supernatural manifestation of the killer was reliving the moment following the murder, looking for clean clothes to replace the bloodstained ones she had committed her murders in.

Residents of the former Blue Ball Inn have continued to claim that strange things happen in the building. Although the old kitchen was converted into a book room, it is still the focus of haunted activity in the house. Recent inhabitants have claimed to hear quick series of knocks coming from the book room. According to one resident, a housekeeper resigned after she felt a freezing-cold hand grab and hold onto her shoulder. Apparently the room was empty, but the grip was so strong it hurt, leaving a bruised imprint where the invisible hand had grabbed the poor woman. Household dogs that have come and gone exhibited extreme dislike for both the book room and Priscilla's old bedroom, growling menacingly with raised hackles into the empty chambers. Other dogs have been seized by sudden fits of inexplicable fear, yelping unexpectedly and running as if from an invisible assailant.

We may never know what moved Priscilla Moore Robinson to commit the atrocious acts attributed to her. Were they revenge for some unknown domestic violence? Perhaps the struggling innkeeper murdered for money, robbing her victims of their possessions before she buried them. Or was she simply a psychopathic murderer living in a time when mental disorders went unrecognized? Given the sparse information we have today, all we can do is guess. But whatever the reasons behind the murders at the Blue Ball Inn, they were obviously inhuman enough to leave an unnatural imprint that has survived new inhabitants, renovations and the passage of over a century.

4
Public
Phantoms

~

If haunted houses are the supernatural domain of domestic drama, and possessed businesses lodge ghosts that belong to the community, then phantoms in public buildings are the ghosts that, in some way or another, define the locale they are from. Whether they dwell in churches, theaters, museums or prisons, the ghosts in these prominent public buildings are usually spectral representations of some significant, dramatic or traumatic event from the building's past.

Unlike most businesses, these buildings are inherently historical, standing as reminders, lessons or examples of our past. The ghosts that haunt them are more than disembodied footsteps, inexplicable cold drafts and shimmering apparitions; they also stand as dynamic history lessons. Usually victims of some locally famous incident, the ghosts and the tales that have grown around them provide us with a glimpse into the world that belonged to them. Here is a handful of ghosts that reside in the public buildings of Pennsylvania, from the menacing shade in Slippery Rock's Old Stone House to the tortured souls lost in the dilapidated halls of Philadelphia's Eastern State Penitentiary. Do not assume that the populated settings of the tales that follow make for bashful phantoms. The ghosts that haunt these public places are seldom shy of strangers.

~

Eastern State Penitentiary

During the early months of 1971, prisoners who had been interned in Philadelphia's Eastern State Penitentiary were moved to the new Graterford Prison located 25 miles northeast of the city. Day by day, week by week, more and more cells in the enormous facility were emptied, leaving behind an intangible oppressiveness that hung in the silence of the huge building. For the last prison guards to walk the crumbling halls of Eastern State, closing day couldn't come soon enough.

Now that the prison wasn't being used anymore, any object that one might find in the foundering hulk of peeling paint, crumbling plaster and rusting metal suddenly seemed imbued with some kind of personality. It was as if the history of the place—the ineffable suffering of the thousands who had been incarcerated there—infused the air with a foreboding hostility that could be felt in every little thing. A rusted red cross ornamenting the gate of the infirmary was somehow transformed into a talisman of evil, dentist chairs no longer in use somehow became instruments of torture, empty cells with splitting mattresses were turned into dens of desolation and the shadows in the long, empty hallways became living things that breathed resentment and hatred.

The last guards to make their rounds through the prison whispered spine-chilling stories to each other—stories about the sounds of pacing and whispers coming from within cells that were obviously empty, about dark shadows resembling people quickly moving down halls and about eerie wails drifting to the ear from somewhere within the immense complex. To those last prison employees who remained behind in Eastern State Penitentiary, it became all too obvious that some other force had taken over the building. The people who had made all the rules in the world-famous house of detention were no longer in charge, and the spirits of those whose combined years of imprisonment made up a frightening count of centuries were determined to make the place theirs.

By the time the building's last living prisoners were removed on April 14, anyone who had spent any time there was certain that something unnatural was afoot in Eastern State Penitentiary. Possessed by a force inherently hostile to humanity, the building had come a long way from the high ideals that marked its origins in the 18th century.

Initially conceived from Quaker philosophies that extolled the benefits of solitary meditation for wayward members of society, the institution's objective was to provide an environment of "solitude, work and penitence" for the prisoners. Admitting its first prisoner in 1829, Eastern State Penitentiary was the first product of prison reform in the United States, a genuine attempt to better the souls of prisoners sentenced to do time within its walls. The first such prison on the continent, it occasioned the induction of the word "penitentiary" (derived from the Quaker and Protestant understanding of spiritual penitence) into the American lexicon. But as years wore on and prisoners accumulated, it became increasingly obvious that nothing holy was occurring inside Eastern State Penitentiary.

It turned out that total isolation was not ideal for many criminals. Men and women imprisoned in Eastern

State were more likely to fester in the crippling conditions of their loneliness than meditate on Christian morality. Hooded whenever they were out of their chambers so that they could not see or be seen, and completely alone while confined in their 8 by 12 foot cells, inmates who were not fighting off the demons of imposed isolation were desperately trying to communicate with other inmates any way they could. Tapping on pipes, whispering into air vents or tossing notes attached to pebbles over the walls of their private exercise areas—prisoners did everything they could to break the divine solitude of Eastern State Penitentiary.

The punishment for communication was severe. Prisoners could be sent into debilitating conniptions of fear if the words "Water Bath," "Mad Chair" or "Iron Gag" were hissed through the feed slots of their thick iron doors. Inmates treated to the Water Bath were dunked in ice-cold water and then hoisted on a wall and left there over an evening. This punishment was usually carried out during the winter months when the water would freeze onto the skin. The Mad Chair torture had individuals tightly strapped into a seat, where they would remain for days, unable to even twitch because of the leather constraints strapped to every appendage. By the time a person was released from the Mad Chair, the lack of circulation would have turned the individual's appendages bluish-black. And then there was the Iron Gag. The most feared of all, this brutal device consisted of an iron collar that was clamped around the individual's tongue and then chained to the wrists, which were bound high and behind the back. The restraints were kept on for days, and every

IMPLEMENTS of TORTURE,
and their Dangerous Effects, Illustrated.
By James Akin, N°18 Prune Street Philadelphia.
Taken from M.daw's detailed statements.

of its natural size, locked upon Mathias Maccumsey,
a convict from Lancaster County, sentenced to the Cells for
Manslaughter, who Died with it in his mouth, in the
Eastern STATE PENITENTIARY, of
PENNSYLVANIA.
June 1833.

In open defiance of all the known maxims of Law, and
contrary to Legislative enactments, a convict is compelled
to endure the appalling tortures of this infernal contrivance,
for merely speaking to a fellow prisoner. In a Land, too, where
Tyranny and Oppression, is held in utter abhorrence, and
Liberty, Equality, and a just enjoyment of rights, are the constant
boasting of the people !!! The Spanish inquisitions, cannot
exhibit a more fearful and barbarous mode, beyond all
human endurance! It ought to be forever abolished !!!

Entered according to Act of Congress, in the Year 1833, by James Akin in the Clerks Office, of the
District Court, of the Eastern District of Pennsylvania.

The Iron Gag, one of several torture devices used at Eastern State Penitentiary

twitch the captor made caused the metal collar to dig into the tongue. The ensuing bleeding in the mouth was severe, and many people died of blood loss after days of this agony.

Such measures weren't part of the system of penitence devised by the Quakers. Instead, they were improvised procedures enacted by the staff manning the jail. These were not the only violations. Unbeknownst to the state, Block 13, constructed in 1925, contained especially small cells that had neither adequate light nor ventilation. Prisoners punished for any number of jailhouse offences would be locked in these substandard rooms. When these cells were discovered years later, inspectors ordered the prison authorities to tear down the walls between them to make bigger chambers. Another chilling discovery by inspectors later on was "the Hole" under Block 14. The pit dug underneath the cellblock was reserved for especially troublesome inmates. These unfortunates would serve weeks among the vermin in the hole, subsisting on one cup of water and one slice of bread per day.

The most commonly documented problem among the inmates at Eastern State was insanity. Whereas prison authorities assumed that the convicts' own actions were leading them down the road to madness, others called the theory of "beneficial solitary confinement" into question. When the great British author Charles Dickens visited the world-famous prison in the early 1840s to write a chapter in his book *American Notes,* he was appalled at the psychological ramifications of the Eastern's methods.

Dickens described the hood that was draped over an inmate's head when he entered the penitentiary as a "dark shroud, an emblem of the curtain dropped between him and the living world." He was convinced that solitary confinement did more harm than good to prisoners, and his accounts of interviews with inmates are loaded with emotional passages. Of the look in the eyes of a man serving a grueling ten-year sentence, Dickens wrote: "He is like a man buried alive, to be dug out in the slow round of years; and in the meantime dead to everything but torturing anxieties and horrible despair."

Another man, so burdened by the steady weight of loneliness pressing down on him over the years, lost himself to a mural he was painting on the walls of his cell. Dickens is said to have caught his breath when he looked on the work, which covered every inch of the prisoner's cell. It was, Dickens claimed, one of the most amazing works of art he had ever seen. But there was no one present to accept his congratulations. Staring at Dickens with a disturbing blankness in his eyes, the man had obviously lost some irretrievable part of his soul to the pigments on his walls. Although the inmate was neither ranting, slobbering nor weeping hysterically, Dickens could had no doubt that the poor soul had gone mad.

The haunting accounts above describe the sorry states of just two men among the thousands of prisoners who did time in Eastern State Penitentiary. That there are countless other stories of loneliness, misery and madness that go untold we can be sure. Indeed, the very walls of Eastern State Penitentiary seem to whisper it. There were so many cases of madness in the prison that one warden's report of affairs in 1892 suggested that some people are simply destined for insanity, that nothing could be done to reduce the alarmingly high incidence of lunacy occurring in Eastern State when so many of the individuals interred there were mentally fragile to begin with. He never once suggested that it may have been the conditions in the prison that drove the prisoners over the brink.

Although there weren't many accounts of strange events when the prison was open, innumerable stories have emerged from within its peeling walls since its closure. Eerie sounds have been heard coming from cells that have been empty for decades. In fact, one of the big draws for many of the visitors touring the prison today is the chance that they might have a supernatural encounter of their own, and a lot of them have not been disappointed. Besides the eerie sounds floating through the building— the giggling, weeping and whispering that have been reported to somehow seep from the very walls—people have spotted dark shadows flitting through the halls.

In one of the older cellblocks, a number of people swear to have seen a dark human silhouette standing still and quiet. Those who have seen this shadow have often claimed to have felt a profound loathing emanating from it, as if the wraith-like form was sustained by hatred alone. Sightings of this shadow have never lasted for very long, for it is known to simply vanish whenever it is directly acknowledged. Individuals who have called out to it—or even defied their own instincts and taken a few steps closer to the malevolent apparition—have more often than not found themselves rubbing their eyes, staring in wonder or even doubting their own sanity. Where one second ago there stood an undeniable presence there was now only the emptiness of a decaying old hallway.

Another of Eastern State Penitentiary's most frequently appearing ghosts is a specter perched high in a guard tower. It has been assumed for many years that this ghost is the spirit of a prison guard, still manning his post years after passing on. It might seem strange to some that an employee, free to leave the walls at the end of the workday, would remain behind in such a dismal place after he died. But we can only guess at what sort of incidents the guard might have witnessed while he worked at Eastern State—

Specters of dead inmates occasionally materialize at Eastern State, perhaps in protest to their inhumane treatment while incarcerated.

events, perhaps, that affected him so deeply that some part of his being was unable to move on after his body expired. Thus he goes on reliving whatever sights, sounds or realizations struck him while posted to the watchtower.

Today, the prison is one of Philadelphia's big tourist attractions. Run by the Pennsylvania Prison Society, Eastern State has become a curiosity for many different groups: those interested in how the penal system developed from its roots in early America, those intrigued by the architecture of incarceration and, of course, those on the lookout for evidence of the supernatural.

The caretakers of Eastern State have tapped into this public fascination for the supernatural. Throughout October 2001, the "Terror Behind the Walls" tour took visitors on a paranormal promenade through the halls of the old prison. Staffed by a full cast playing deceased police officers and lunatic inmates, coupled with boisterous special effects and over-the-top lighting, the show at the closed-down prison made most other Halloween haunted houses seem modest in comparison.

Screams echoed through the halls of Eastern State during the month of October as startled visitors walked through corridors lined with garishly made-up ghouls clutching at them and three-dimensional images of light flashing through the air. Yet supernatural enthusiasts will readily concur that even this show was a mere caricature of the real ghostly events that take place in the prison. For it is after the clamor of imitation subsides, when the only noise to be heard in the penitentiary is the wind whistling through the stonework or an iron grate creaking slightly open somewhere, that the true ghosts of Eastern State come out to be seen. It is during these moments that the horrible weight of the building's past creeps out under cover of night, looking for some sort of expression in the grand desolation of the deserted penitentiary.

The Mishler Theater

On February 15, 1906, magic came to the town of Altoona. That was the date that the doors of the Mishler Theater swung open to the public for the first time. The hard-working citizens of the fledgling railroad town were treated to a spectacle that, for the most part, could be experienced only in the country's big metropolitan centers. Today, we can only imagine the buzz in the air and the awe of the crowd as they walked into the brand-new theater's opulent auditorium for the first time. The ironwork, terra-cotta and glass were ordered in from Philadelphia, the marble and mosaics were commissioned from the best artists in Pittsburgh and the box chairs came from Vienna, Austria. It was luxury the likes of which Altoona had never seen, and, thanks to Isaac Charles Mishler, it was here to stay.

Like so many others who lived in Altoona, Isaac Mishler came to the young borough as an employee of the Pennsylvania Railroad when the company was expanding its line from Philadelphia to Pittsburgh. Barely 19 years old when he arrived in town, Mishler worked for the railroad for eight more years before opening his own cigar shop in downtown Altoona. Mishler's knack with people and love of baseball turned his store into a common meeting place for baseball fans in and around town. It was not long before Isaac became an active member of the baseball community, bringing a good number of ball teams into the Pennsylvania State League.

But the theater was Mishler's first love. He took over the management of the Eleventh Avenue Opera House in

The impressive façade of the Mishler Theater in Altoona

1893, booking and promoting shows in the modest venue, which he would continue to do until the theater burnt down in 1907. While construction crews were building Mishler, the new theater that was to bear his name, the impresario broadened his experience in the business. For a short time he also ran the Cambria Theater in Johnstown, Pennsylvania, and the State Street Theater in Trenton, New Jersey.

So it was that when the Mishler Theater opened for business the day after Valentine's Day in 1906, Isaac Mishler was well acquainted with what it took to run a theater. And by all accounts, he was successful in keeping the enormous 1900-seat venue booked with high-quality theatrical productions. The theater served as the first stop for traveling shows that started in Philadelphia or New York. Critics paid close attention to how the Mishler audiences received these productions, gauging a show's potential on the road by how the Altoona audience reacted to it.

In November 1906, only nine months after the Mishler Theater opened, a fire that started in a building across the alley spread to the theater. By the time it was put out, the flame had virtually gutted Mishler's pride and joy, incinerating all the classical finery adorning the building's interior. If Mishler gave up any time to despair, his public statements did not show it. The theater's proprietor reacted quickly and emphatically. Although he was short on funds to carry out the repairs, Mishler would do everything he could to restore the theater to its former splendor. With local citizens guaranteeing the capital to rebuild the theater and crews working around the clock seven days a week, the Mishler Theater reopened on January 21, 1907, a remarkable three months after the building was ravaged by fire.

Isaac Mishler would be rewarded for his resolve: the next 15 years were to be the theater's golden age. Legendary performers such as George Raft, Helen Hayes, Isadora Duncan, George Jessel, Al Jolsen, Ed Wynn, W.C. Fields, Ethel Barrymore and Sarah Bernhardt all walked the stage at the Mishler Theater. Business thrived for Isaac during the early 20th century. But Isaac saw the coming shift toward movies and began modifying the theater to accommodate films as early as 1912. However, as celluloid replaced stage shows, it became ever more difficult to book live performances. Mishler finally capitulated to the dawning era of film in 1923, selling his theater to a man named A. Notopoulos, who made it into a dedicated movie house.

The historic building would have more than its share of trials throughout the rest of the 20th century, enduring waning popularity and, in 1965, a bid to flatten it into a parking lot, followed by a number of preservation movements. It is estimated that since 1969, over $1.3 million has been spent in restoring the old building. A considerable sum, no doubt, but people who know the Mishler Theater understand that its value lies apart from the dollar sums attached to it, beyond the physical labor put into its restoration and even beyond its historical cultural relevance. For, according to more than one paranormal expert, the Mishler Theater is not only one of Blair County's most prized historical sites, it also one of the county's most haunted buildings as well.

One of the most common supernatural events to occur in the Mishler takes place in the first balcony box at stage right. It is there that actors on-stage have often seen none other than Isaac Mishler himself, dressed in a trim black suit, with his dark moustache combed and hair carefully styled, silently watching the performances he loved so much while he was alive. It is widely believed that he frequently appears there because his office used to be located right next to that balcony, and it was from that vantage point that he would most often watch actors rehearse. But the old patron of the building has been seen in other locations as well—staring blankly from the galleries above the stage, slowly walking the catwalk and idly sitting in the dressing-room area. It has become obvious to those that frequent the theater that Isaac Mishler signed away only the title deed when he sold the theater those many years ago. His heart, however, never left the theater, remaining behind even after the man himself passed on.

Additional evidence suggests that Isaac Mishler is not the only man who developed a strong attachment for the theater while he was alive. Legend has it that two caretakers who used to work in the magnificent building slowly fell in love with the place while they worked alone during the evening's quiet hours. So much so, in fact, that they requested their ashes be discreetly spread through the theater after they were gone. The request was faithfully fulfilled by the caretakers' families.

Many people believe that these two caretakers haunt the theater along with its first proprietor. However, the activities associated with the caretakers tend to be more mischievous in nature than the rather austere appearances by Isaac Mishler himself.

On more than one occasion, directors who have been watching rehearsals from the audience seats have felt someone tapping them quickly on the shoulder, only to turn around and see rows of empty seats stretching into the darkened room behind them. One evening, the director and co-producer of a play were in the theater late, sitting near the front of the stage, looking over their notes for the upcoming production. The only other person in the building was Merle, the caretaker at the time, who was going about his nightly duties.

The two men were snapped out of their theatrical discussion when the sound of footsteps on-stage reminded them how late it was getting. Under the fringes of the stage curtain, which were about one foot off the ground, they could see feet moving steadily across the stage. "Hey Merle," the director called out, "we'll be out of here in just a couple of minutes, OK?"

"Fine, no problem," Merle yelled out in response from somewhere in the lobby behind them. Both men froze when it dawned on them that Merle was in the lobby and that the pair of feet visible under the stage curtain thus belonged to a fourth person.

The director and co-producer called out to the person behind the curtain. There was only silence. Carefully approaching the stage, both men threw back the curtain to confront the late-night intruder, but there was nobody there. With Merle's help, they combed the Mishler Theater from top to bottom, yet no trace of the man was found. Whoever the two men had seen walking across the stage had simply vanished.

Scott Crownover is a devotee of the theater, a local actor who has done numerous shows in the Mishler. He is also an active member of the Paranormal Research Foundation. His familiarity with supernatural phenomenon, combined with his extensive knowledge of the Mishler Theater, makes him something of an expert on the ghosts in the building.

A theatrical colleague of Crownover's once asked him if the foundation would be willing to investigate the theater's second balcony. It was there, in a part of the building yet to be touched by any preservation work, that several people operating spotlights have been touched by invisible hands. Lighting technicians would feel the hands while tracking actors across the stage with the follow-spots—a gentle tap here, a sudden grab there. It was more than some of the stagehands could bear. Crownover would have been happy to have the foundation he belonged to investigate, but the production's director believed that the presence of ghost hunters would distract the people on the lights, so they were left to deal with the mischievous spirits on their own.

The Paranormal Research Foundation eventually did conduct an investigation in the Mishler Theater. And though they were not able to find any evidence of spirits on the second balcony, the team did come up with some dramatic findings in other parts of the building that night. An infrared video camera set up on the famous first balcony box at stage right—where the spirit of Isaac Mishler had been so often spotted by actors on-stage—captured the image of a dark shadow slowly moving across the box.

In one of their photographs, the foundation also picked up the image of an orb of light hovering in the middle of a staircase in the theater. It turned out that a woman had once tumbled down this very staircase after being seized by a fatal heart attack in the middle of a show. The story goes that the theater staff didn't want to interrupt the show, so they lifted her out of the theater to the ambulance, telling anyone who asked that she had broken a limb and had been sedated. The show went on undisturbed that night, but it appears likely that some part of the woman's essence remained behind in the building, yet another ghost in the already quite haunted Mishler Theater.

Today, the Mishler stands as an inspiring example to those who respect the value of the past. Saved from destruction in 1965, the Mishler underwent subsequent restorations sponsored by the Blair County Art Foundation, which have restored it to much of its former glory.

The theater's opulent grandeur is impressive in itself, but some curious visitors might see more in it than extravagant early 20th-century design. From underneath the gold-fringed columns and the carefully carved Muses watching over the theater's exterior shines the all-too-obvious reverence the builders felt for their subject. In the carefully wrought lavishness of the Mishler Theater, we may catch a glimpse of America's future adoration for the entertainment industry as a whole. Decades before movie stars would be counted among society's most respected members and Los Angeles would become the destination for millions of Hollywood hopefuls, dramatic venues such as Altoona's Mishler Theater were whispering of humanity's powerful need for escape. From William Shakespeare to Bruce Willis, the more things change, the more they stay the same. Perhaps this is what Isaac Mishler is saying with his stoic gaze as he watches actors perform from his first balcony box today.

A Ghostly Penitence

On most nights during the spring of 1937, Maxo Vanka could be found inside St. Nicholas Church in Millvale on the northern outskirts of Pittsburgh. The world-famous artist spent most of his waking hours perched upon scaffolding set up alongside the old Croatian church's interior walls, bent on making life spring from their unadorned surfaces. According to more than a few art lovers, he came as close to succeeding in this endeavor as any other painter who came before or after him. The masterpiece mural that Maxo Vanka created is one of the best-known in the country.

Mixing Marxist ideas of social justice with traditional Christian imagery, the mural aroused much controversy. Depicting the Virgin Mary and the Stations of the Cross alongside venal materialists, greedy stockbrokers and modern-day soldiers, the mural is not typical iconography. Controversial material, but Vanka was a passionate man who had no qualms about mixing religion with politics. "Every man who comes to America from the European cemetery," stated Vanka soon after he fled his native Croatia before the outset of the Second World War, "should show his gratitude to his adopted land by making a contribution to its culture. This church will be mine."

It is clear to anyone who has visited St. Nicholas that Maxo Vanka was inspired. Yet anyone who is familiar with the story of the mural in St. Nicholas will also know that Vanka wasn't inspired solely by political ideology and Christian morality when he was painting. For though he did not know it when he started, Maxo was

Late at night, while Maxo Vanka labored away on this breathtaking mural, the apparition of a dead priest would materialize.

commissioned to work in a haunted house of God. More than once, the mysterious ghost that was rumored to drift through the aisles of St. Nicholas came to pay the artist a visit. Indeed, it was his experiences with the ghost in the church, documented by his good friend Louis Adamic in a 1938 edition of *Harper's Magazine,* that would turn the holy building into one of Pennsylvania's most famous haunted sites.

The atmosphere Vanka was working in was definitely conducive to supernatural encounters. Alone in an old church late into the night, carefully brushing in the details of holy figures by the light of a lantern as the scaffolding creaks and the wind howls, one might expect to see all sorts of things in the long shadows of the old church. But Vanka, not a man of superstitious inclinations, was able to conceive of all sorts of rational explanations for the things he was seeing inside St. Nicholas.

Vanka's faith in his rational faculties was first tested after his fourth night in the church. The dogs kept outside the rectory gave the first sign that something odd was happening. The two animals were unusually loud, barking and yelping as Maxo worked that night. The painter shut out the noise and continued to work. Not much later, he would see the mysterious figure for the first time.

In his 1938 *Harper's* article, Louis Adamic quoted Vanka: "While mixing paint and feeling rather cold and tired but not exhausted, I glanced at the altar beneath me, which was rather fully illuminated by my lamp's down-ward flood of light…and there was a figure, a man in black, moving this way and that way in front of it, raising his arms and making gestures in the air."

Too preoccupied with his work to pay the figure much attention, the artist just assumed that it was Father Zagar, the priest who had commissioned the mural, blessing the altar or conducting some other priestly rite. If it was odd that the priest did not say a word to the artist working up above, Vanka did not think too much about it.

"That night," Vanka is quoted as saying, "I quit shortly after two o'clock. As I got out of the church, the dogs, which had been barking violently during the past several hours, dashed up to me, terribly excited." Licking his hands, pawing at him and barking, the dogs were obviously anxious about something that Vanka could only guess at. He did not equate the animals' enthusiasm with anything supernatural.

After each of the artist's painting sessions, Father Zagar had taken to meeting Vanka for a late-night coffee and cake. Sometime in their conversation that night, Vanka brought up the nocturnal blessings, asking the pastor what he had been doing at the altar so late. Zagar looked at Vanka for a long time before speaking. "That was not me," was all the priest said, and their chat was over for the night.

Four nights later, while Maxo was still painting above the altar, a strange chill crept over his body. Looking down from where he worked on the scaffolding, Vanka spotted the silent man again. He was dressed in black and standing behind the altar. The man's lips were moving, and he was gesturing rather dramatically with his arms, apparently placing some sort of blessing on the empty church. This time Maxo had to work to convince himself that the man below was Father Zagar, and he deliberately went back to putting the finishing touches on the Madonna above the altar.

Some time later that evening, he heard slow footsteps walking somewhere down below. Vanka looked down through the darkness of the church to see the lone figure once again. This time he was moving slowly down the center aisle dividing the pews. Although the man's face was obscured by the low light, Vanka could tell that his lips were moving rhythmically—and there was an indistinct murmur was coming from them.

The sight of the man made Vanka uneasy, but the artist once again tried to convince himself that the figure was Father Zagar and tried to get back to work. That was when the man in black walked underneath him and cut out all the lights below the scaffolding. Except for the light emanating from the lantern Vanka kept by him, the interior of the church was instantly black. Clutching tightly to his lantern, Vanka stared into the thick darkness, listening to the two parish-house dogs howling desperately outside.

It was about half past midnight when Vanka decided to visit Father Zagar, intent on discovering why the man had killed the lights while he was painting. Finding Zagar asleep in the rectory, Vanka assumed that the priest was a sleepwalker. The artist woke him up, telling him about what had just transpired in the church. Father Zagar looked troubled as he assured Vanka that he had never sleepwalked in his life. Furthermore, something in his voice confirmed all of Maxo's doubts regarding his own rationalizations.

"Well, then, who was it?" Vanka asked.

Father Zagar looked at Vanka gravely for a moment before speaking. "Tell me," the priest began, "have you since coming here heard there is a tradition that this church is occasionally visited by a ghost or some strange phenomenon?"

"No," Maxo replied.

"Are you sure?"

"Yes."

Father Zagar sat in silence for a few moments, wondering how, or if, he should continue. "Well then," he said, finally breaking the stifling silence, "let me tell you about the story of St. Nicholas. People began to whisper of the ghost in this church about 15 years ago—nine or ten years before I became pastor. Personally, I have never had any experience with him, or it, but there are others, many others, who say that they have. Years before I came here, there were fights among the Croatians about this ghost, spirit, whatever it is. I have always been skeptical about such things, but the way people have spoken of it, there are times when I feel that maybe there are some phenomena we might not understand."

As Maxo Vanka sat there in silence, thinking about what Father Zagar had just told him, the pastor continued speaking. "Do you know why I've always been up so late to meet with you after every night's work?"

"No," said Vanka. "Why?"

"Because," replied the priest, "since you started working late, I was frightened that you might see something in the church that would frighten you so badly you might fall from the scaffolding. So I have been watching over you from behind a door, being careful not to disturb you, but there nevertheless so that I might come to your aid should you fall. Tonight was the only evening I was too tired to keep up my vigil. You found me asleep."

"Father," Vanka said after Zagar was finished, a smile creeping across his face, "you aren't crazy, are you?"

Zagar laughed. "That is another thing I'm not so sure about."

The mood lightened, and the two men had coffee and cake, resolving that from that night on, Father Zagar would openly stay in the church while Maxo painted.

The mood was lively the next night. Both men were laughing loudly as Vanka painted, making jokes about the legendary specter that had supposedly been haunting St. Nicholas. A little bit of company did much to alleviate the vague foreboding that Vanka had been feeling about the project since he had first seen the black figure.

Father Zagar even went so far as to mockingly invoke his powers as a man of the cloth, demanding that the stray spirit appear before them. No sooner had the last words of Zagar's holy evocation echoed through the church than something in the air changed. In the silence that followed, both men were suddenly filled with a deep feeling of foreboding. It was then that a single knock from somewhere in the back of the church filled the room. There was another knock, followed by another and another. It was obvious to both that there was something in the church with them. In the next instant, the two dogs kept by the parish house began barking wildly outside.

Father Zagar called on his powers again, but this time there was little humor in his voice. "Be you a ghost or a dead man, go with God," the priest cried into the air. "May you rest in peace," he continued. "I shall pray for you, just please leave us be."

Vanka cut off Zagar's plea, yelling out to the priest as his eyes fell on the fourth pew from the altar. There, staring blankly up at the scaffolding where Maxo was standing, sat the man in black. It was the first time he got a clear look at the man's facial features. He would later describe the way the man looked to Louis Adamic: dressed in black, the apparition was an old man whose bony, wrinkled face was etched into a look of absolute misery. Somehow his skin was colored with a dark bluish tinge. He sat there for just an instant before vanishing into thin air. Zagar spun around violently when Vanka yelled, but he wasn't able to see anything. The man in black was gone before the priest could take a good look.

Meanwhile, up on the scaffolding, Maxo Vanka had gone cold. Something about the sighting on this night had filled him with a fear he had never felt before. His legs shook as he tried to make his way down the scaffolding, trembling so badly that he almost fell from the ladder as he was descending. Uncertain of what to say about his vision, Vanka told the priest that he must have imagined something. The artist was too shaken to continue, and he called it a night, retiring early to a fitful sleep racked with troubled dreams of an old man dressed in black, staring silently with sightless eyes. If he had begun to entertain the possibility that he may have been going mad, Vanka must have been relieved at what Father Zagar would have to say to him the next evening.

The priest, it turned out, had been kept up through the previous night, frightened by the strange noises that he had heard in his room. They were the same sounds that both Vanka and Zagar had heard in the church just before Vanka had seen the ghost. "Something about those sounds filled my bones with a deep, dead cold," the priest confided to his new friend. "I was scared, Maxo. I could not see anything in the darkness, but I knew there was a dead man there, standing just beyond my bed."

That night, while Vanka continued painting, Father Zagar prayed silently, asking that the ghost not bother

Vanka while he was painting. He also requested that the spirit of the old man be given rest.

For the next several nights, it seemed like Zagar's supplications had worked, and the two men filled the evenings with lively conversation, talking about the homes they had left behind in Croatia, the troubles in Europe, their hopes for the future. A few such evenings passed before Father Zagar and Vanka felt comfortable enough to talk about the old man in black. Only then did Zagar tell Vanka what the members of the community believed about the old man that haunted St. Nicholas.

Rumor had it that the church's financial problems stemmed in part from a corrupt pastor's tenure at the old church a number of years previously. The priest had not been a good man, and people suspected that he had pilfered money from the parish while also failing to keep up with his holy duties. It was said that he had remained behind in the church after his death, somehow hoping to make up in death for the sinful indiscretions he had committed while alive. The parishioners did not wish to have anything to do with the former priest's repentant ghost, and it was an unwritten rule in the community that no one should venture into the church after dark, Father Zagar concluded.

It turned out that Father Zagar's prayers were not sufficient to free the phantom priest from his earthly obligations after all. About a week had passed uneventfully when the dogs began barking outside, knocks were heard from the back of the church and the two men were beset by fierce chills—then the old man appeared again. However, Vanka was the only one who could see the ghost as he walked down the aisle, approaching the altar with slow, deliberate steps.

Vanka called to Father Zagar, telling his friend that the ghost was back, pointing out where he was. Father Zagar couldn't see the ghost as he approached the sacred flame located on the church altar. Nor did he see the dead priest cup his hands around the protected candle and blow gently, but he plainly saw the candle go out. Father Zagar let out a cry of alarm as the sacred flame—which had not been extinguished once since the day it had been lit over eight years ago—went out. A glass bulb, designed to protect the flame from any breezes or drafts, sat atop the light, but apparently it was not of much use where the supernatural was concerned. And indeed, without a shadow of a doubt, something supernatural was afoot in St. Nicholas.

The ghostly priest continued to appear throughout the spring and into early summer as Vanka worked on his murals. Maxo's encounters with the man in black would always begin the same way: with a deep and sudden chill. Shortly after he was seized by the cold, Vanka would inevitably see the deceased priest within the church. Sometimes the spirit would be busy lighting candles; on other occasions he seemed to be wandering aimlessly through the aisles or sitting at one of the pews, staring blankly at the altar.

The dead priest's actions were innocuous enough, but there was something about him that filled Vanka with absolute dread. "He looked perfectly mild, pensive-like, sitting in the pew or moving up and down the aisle; yet he filled me with indescribable horror, with something higher and stronger than fear—what, I cannot tell you," the artist later explained to Louis Adamic.

Each time, Vanka would try to ignore the chills and the sight of the ghost and continue to paint, but he found it almost impossible to focus. Instead, he would quit for the night soon after the ghost appeared. Despite the dead priest and the resulting shortened working nights, Vanka finished the mural in about two months, leaving St. Nicholas with some of the most splendid artwork in the country.

As impressive as Vanka's painting turned out, the ghost in St. Nicholas stole much of the press' attention from the famous Croatian artist. After Adamic's article was published in *Harper's,* a swarm of local journalists flooded to St. Nicholas in search of the dead priest. A lot of newspaper writers kept lengthy midnight watches, hoping to catch sight of the spirit that had haunted Maxo Vanka while he worked, but none of them would ever be able to write a firsthand account of the man in black.

Subsequent priests at St. Nicholas have expressed dismay that the ghost in St. Nicholas has received more attention than Vanka's murals. It might seem ironic that the story of a ghost seen by one man so many years ago would garner more publicity than a splendid mural exhibited every day for all to see. Whatever the case, it seems that Vanka's artwork in St. Nicholas is finally starting to attract the public's esteem.

The Gift of Sympathy: The Art of Maxo Vanka, an art exhibit celebrating the work of the Croatian artist, was recently featured in a number of art galleries and museums in Pennsylvania. The exhibit has sparked a renewed appreciation for the murals in Millvale's St.

Nicholas Church, resulting in more visitors than ever before. It seems that the legend of the man in black has finally been overshadowed by the sheer brilliance of Vanka's masterpiece. Yet who knows when the mysterious ghost that haunted Maxo Vanka so many years ago will once more appear before human eyes, sadly trudging up and down the church aisles, perhaps seeking atonement for the vices that corrupted him while he was still living?

The Portrait of Nellie Tallman

Nellie Tallman was perched high on the stool, trying hard to remain still. But the fancy chiffon dress she was draped in was not the most comfortable garment. And, however strict her Victorian upbringing, the three-year-old child was subject to the same bouts of restlessness that afflict all children her age. Morning turned into afternoon, and the young girl's rigid posture deteriorated into a mess of shifting, scratching and stretching as the hours passed.

The year was 1870. Nellie's father, John Tallman, stood on the other side of the room, looking from where his daughter sat to the canvas stretched before him, concentrating, trying hard to select those colors from the pallet that would best capture the blush on his fidgety subject's face.

Neither father nor daughter had any way of knowing that they were teetering on the brink of tragedy. Little did they suspect that the next moment would burn a scar on the Tallman family and give rise to one of Lycoming County's most lasting legends. In the space of a single brushstroke, Nellie's restless shifting set her off balance, and an instant later she was tumbling backward from her high seat. The unfortunate girl broke her neck when she hit the ground. She was dead in three days.

Although many of us might consider the portrait a morbid memento of Nellie's last moments, the grief-stricken Mr. Tallman cherished the painting. He perceived something in it—some part of his beloved daughter that had survived the gruesome fall—and insisted on finishing it and displaying it in his home. Time would prove that Mr. Tallman was right. From the beginning, it was obvious that the portrait was no ordinary painting.

John Tallman, who had been tutored by the famous still-life artist Severin Roesen, could hardly be called one of America's great artists, but there is something extraordinary about his portrait of Nellie. Some viewers have commented on the luminosity of her skin, others on the unsettling sentience in her eyes, almost as if a living energy emanated from the pigments within the oval frame. But if the painting truly did embody a part of Nellie Tallman's departed soul, she must have been a shy girl, because whenever her likeness has been hung up for show, the portrait seems to have done everything it could to get off the wall.

Nellie's portrait cooperated with no one, not even her father. No matter how many times he hung the painting up, on whatever wall, with whatever hanging fixture, without fail he would find the painting of his daughter

This portrait of Nellie Tallman, completed by her father after her accidental death, is possessed by the spirit of the three-old-year girl.

face down on the floor when he saw it next. After a number of failed attempts at keeping the canvas up, John conceded that his daughter's face would not grace his home, and he stored the painting away in the attic.

Years passed, generations came and went, and Nellie Tallman remained undisturbed in the dark confines of the attic. It wasn't until the early 1970s, when family descendents decided to sell the home, that the portrait was rediscovered. The Tallmans offered the painting to the Lycoming County Historical Museum in Williamsport, and Nellie was once more hoisted onto a wall before the public. The light of day would have revealed a completely different world to the innocent eyes of the perpetually young girl. Cars, clothes, airplanes, television—though her new surroundings were completely unrecognizable, the spirit of the child was still intent on playing her old games.

Disaster struck on the first night that Nellie's portrait hung in the Williamsport museum. A car came tearing down Maynard Street, barreled through the stop sign in front of the museum and crashed through the front of the building. Continuing on its freakish trajectory, the automobile did not stop until it had exited the museum through the back. Regardless of what the incident was—coincidence, bad driving, bad luck or something else—amid the wreck the painting of Nellie, which had been hung from the ceiling, was found unscathed, lying face down on the floor. Although it might be a bit imprudent to blame Nellie for such destruction, it is hard to ignore that this dramatic event took place on the same day that the tragic portrait emerged after being stored in the Tallman attic for 100 years.

It did not stop there. The museum was restored and the painting was hung back up, but Nellie was apparently still not happy about being there. More than one visitor reported feeling uncomfortable under the stern gaze of the three-year-old child. And no matter what efforts the museum staff made to keep the painting mounted, Nellie always found a way to confound them. When her image was moved to the Victorian Parlor, a security system was set up so that any movement near her painting would set off an alarm. Nevertheless, when the staff returned the next morning, Nellie's portrait was found flat on the sofa on the other side of the room.

Nellie continued to disappoint custodians, repeatedly falling down from where she had been hung when nobody was looking. Until, that is, her painting was put up across the room from a piece done by Severin Roesen. Perhaps she recognizes the work of her father's famous mentor and has been quieted by the memory of John Tallman. Or maybe she's content to look at a vibrant still life painted by one of the masters. Whatever the case, Nellie Tallman has been well behaved for the past few years, hanging high off the floor, as still as we would expect an inanimate object to be. However, many people passing through the doors of the Lycoming County Historical Museum have reported a disturbing feeling when walking too close to the girl's portrait—as if, they claimed, they were being watched.

Old Stone House

Dr. David Dixon had just been appointed curator of the Old Stone House, and he had made it his business to know everything there was to know about the 19th-century building. David had no training, experience or affinity for the supernatural, and so initially he wasn't sure how to take the odd stories that were circulating about the Old Stone House. He first learned of the strange goings-on in the historic inn when a young park warden came in to visit late one day in the summer of 1992. As learned as Dr. Dixon thought he was about the old building, there were some things about the house not covered in the local histories.

So it happened that the jittery and visibly distracted park warden became the first person to inform Dr. Dixon of its unofficial history. It turned out that the woman used to work at the Old Stone House as a tour guide when it was still under the management of the Pennsylvania Historical and Museum Commission, and she had decided to drop by late that day to see if anything had changed since she had worked there. She seemed uneasy, as if she wanted to ask Dr. Dixon about the place but wasn't sure where to start. Standing in front of the curator, uncertain of how to say what she wanted to say, she settled for the innocuous question, "Can I take a look around?"

"Yup," Dr. Dixon replied, "you've got a few minutes while I close up."

Only after she took herself through a short tour of the house did she return to where Dr. Dixon was finishing his closing duties. This time, she was determined to speak. "Can I tell you something?" the woman asked.

Dr. Dixon interrupted his work and looked over at the nervous young visitor. "Sure," he replied.

"Well," she haltingly began, "when I worked here, I always had this…sense…that there was some kind of presence here."

David knew that stories about "sensing some kind of presence" always led to one topic—ghosts. A trained social scientist, he was immediately skeptical, but he let his guest carry on.

"One night," the woman continued, "I was closing the place up. Everything was cleaned and squared away, and when I locked up, there was definitely no one in the house." The park warden stopped there, not sure how to continue. "The next day," she began again, prosaically enough, "I had the opening shift and was the first one to arrive."

She explained that she had gone through the place quickly, just to make sure that everything in the house was ready for the first tour of the day. It was in the tavern room, she said, that her eyes fell on a sight that made her freeze in mute terror. There, on the antique gaming table was something that sent a chill to her very bones. The dominoes that had been scattered across the table when had she left the night before were now neatly and deliberately arranged to form a single message. They spelled, "GET OUT."

The young guide had been so spooked by this message that she had quit working in the Old Stone House soon afterward. Instead, she had gotten work with one of the other state parks.

Although Dr. Dixon was skeptical about the young woman's story, there was something about her manner that made him think twice. The Slippery Rock University history professor would eventually evaluate her account from the same angle that he did many things—from a historical perspective. He had to admit that the Old Stone House had a dark enough past to warrant the presence of resentful revenants even today.

"The house was built in 1822 by a man named John Brown and initially served as a stagecoach stop, tavern and inn," Dr. Dixon explains. Brown recognized the need for a stopping point on what was then known as the Venango Trail, the road that linked Pittsburgh to all destinations north. The Old Stone House, located roughly halfway between Pittsburgh and Erie, became one of the only safe havens for teamsters working the trail. It was among the first business establishments in the area. The kind of crowd the inn attracted was decidedly frontier—coarse, tough and dangerous—willing to brave hard living conditions and hostile American Indians to make a buck.

A number of criminal operations were headquartered in the Old Stone House over the years. The Stone House Gang was a group of highwaymen who named themselves after the building in which they spent most of their ill-gotten gains. Two separate bands of counterfeiters also made the inn their center of operations when wildcat banks were providing the criminally inclined with a number of good ideas about to how to print currency for nothing. But, as Dr. Dixon recounts, the worst event associated with the Old Stone House occurred one evening in

June 1843, when a Seneca man committed the unspeakable after getting sauced up on the local brew.

Sam Mohawk, a raftsman on the Allegheny River,was on his way back to his reservation after floating logs down the river to Pittsburgh when he stopped in for a visit at the Old Stone House. "He was either intoxicated when he arrived there or became intoxicated at the Old Stone House," Dr. Dixon explains. "Presumably, he became belligerent, and was thrown out of the house by the tavern keeper, at that time a man by the name of John Sill."

"Sam spent the remainder of the night in the woods," Dr. Dixon continues. "He got up before dawn the next morning, got on the road heading north and approached the first farmhouse he saw, a plot owned by a man named James Wigton. Sam Mohawk went into Wigton's house and proceeded to bludgeon to death Mr. Wigton's wife and his five children while James was out working the fields."

The slaughter would go down as one of the worst crimes in Butler County history. "The Indian was apprehended later on that afternoon," Dr. Dixon concludes, "and was taken to the Butler courthouse, where he was eventually tried and executed by hanging."

For an academic historian, the hard past of the Old Stone House might be an excellent case study of the type of business establishments that existed in frontier America. It might inspire a graduate student to write a comparative analysis of the rough characters and violent incidents associated with the Old Stone House and later frontier businesses such as the Long Branch Saloon in Dodge City or the Bull's Head in Abilene. But for ghost enthusiasts, the house's disquieting past provides rich ground for an entirely different sort of inquiry.

Although Dr. David Dixon's doctorate in history might impel him to discuss the historic building's past, he can no longer deny the supernatural buzz about the building in his charge. Indeed, the visiting park warden's ghost story about the Old Stone House would not be the last one he would hear. Far from it.

Since Slippery Rock University had taken over management of the museum in 1983, Dr. Dixon learned that countless additional stories had been circulating. "Seldom does a tour season go by," Dr. Dixon says, "that there aren't bizarre incidents reported at the house."

More often than not, it was the students working in the building as guides who witnessed the strange occurrences. "It happens about three or four times a year," Dr. Dixon says, "where I'll come in to check on them, and they'll tell me that they heard someone walking up the stairs when they were in the office. They'd go running up to see if the visitor wanted a tour, and there'd be nobody there. Every single year since I started in 1992," says an adamant Dr. Dixon, "I've had that same story related to me by different groups of students who have worked there as tour guides."

And students are not the only ones who have witnessed strange occurrences at the museum. "Two years ago [in 1999], we had a Civil War encampment at the Old Stone House," Dr. Dixon remembers. "One of the women who was part of the Civil War reenactment group came up to me and said, 'Do you know that your house is haunted?'"

Dr. Dixon had been working there for the better part of a decade by this time, but he was still somewhat reluctant to endorse the supernatural stories in the house. "Yes," he replied hesitantly, "we have heard stories about that."

"Well," the woman responded, "I saw her this afternoon in one of the bedrooms in the upstairs of the house." This was the first time Dr. Dixon heard someone give a physical description of a spirit in the house. The visitor proceeded to describe the female apparition in detail, from the patterns in her 19th-century dress to the etching in her brooch.

As tempted as the Slippery Rock history professor may have been to dismiss the sighting as the product of an overactive imagination, the woman's story was corroborated by more solid evidence a year later. "In the philosophy department of the university, there is a professor who teaches a course called Mysticism and Psychic Research," Dr. Dixon recalls. "What he wanted to do was to send the students out into the community to investigate stories of hauntings. And so he asked me if I would allow for students to come in and spend the night at the Old Stone House with video cameras, tape recorders and other paraphernalia."

Dr. Dixon gave his permission. The next morning, thanks to the technology of audio recording, after roughly eight years of working there, the curator of the Old Stone House would finally hear evidence of the ghostly intruder. "The students told me that it was a pretty quiet night," Dr. Dixon relates, "but at one point late in the evening, they distinctly heard a kind of shuffling noise in one of the rooms upstairs. They checked the tape recorders on the second floor the next morning, and one of them did capture distinct sounds, which I would probably describe as groaning noises."

These noises were recorded in the same bedroom in which the woman had reported seeing the female apparition a year previous.

Are the footsteps on the stairs, the ghostly apparition that appeared on the second floor and the groans recorded late at night all manifestations of the same spirit? Certainly the question is up for speculation. Is this the spirit of Mrs. Wigton, so savagely murdered by a Seneca intruder years ago? Or are there a number of ghosts still residing in the Old Stone House? Perhaps the high level of supernatural activity in the historic building is a product of the tumultuous past in what was once a wild Butler County. And perhaps it is here that history's forgotten casualties have decided to congregate.

As is usually the case where the supernatural is concerned, no one can say for sure whose spirits are responsible. Meanwhile, things continue as they always have at the Old Stone House—mysterious footsteps echo on the stairs, groans are let out in the middle of the night and a female apparition continues to make her presence known.

5
Spirits
of the
Countryside

~

For the first people who lived in Pennsylvania, the countryside was the state. Whether they were Indians, early colonials or 19th-century homesteaders, most early Americans existed in a close relationship with the land. The roads, rivers, valleys, hills and forests of the state had a direct impact on the day-to-day lives of Pennsylvanians. This fact is lost on many of us today; we live in a society that is largely defined by an urban culture. The daily activities of most people in Philadelphia, Pittsburgh or Scranton rarely involve a single consideration of the surrounding environment, so separate have the cities become from the countryside in the public consciousness.

The ghosts in the following chapter are some of the rural spirits of Pennsylvania—those phantoms that belong to the small towns, hills, forests, rivers and highways of the Keystone State. Here are five tales that attest to the power of the dead to survive after their bodies expire.

~

Ghost Tours of New Hope

Given her lifelong interest in the supernatural, Adele Gamble couldn't be living in a better place. The town of New Hope, with its Georgian architecture, lush scenery and thriving arts scene, has roots that reach back to the early 18th century—a time when the United States was just 13 colonies huddling against the Atlantic Ocean. As with so many places imbued with a lengthy history, there is more to New Hope than meets the eye. This extra dimension exists just beyond sensory impression, lingering somewhere in the intangible, saturating the distinct colonial air of the place with the feeling that ghosts are nearby. New Hope's streets are full of them. The incidence of haunting is so high in the old town that prolific ghostwriter Charles J. Adams III has gone on record to say that New Hope might be the "most haunted place in Pennsylvania, if not the world."

Adele Gamble wouldn't have it any other way. For as long as she can remember, she has been sensitive to those intangibles that her town has in abundance. Her early abilities were limited to modest precognition, such as knowledge of who was on the other end of a ringing phone or doorbell before she answered. Yet her sixth sense developed as she grew older, culminating with her first sighting of an actual ghost some 30 years ago.

"It was when my ex-father-in-law passed away," Adele recalls. "He appeared to me after he died." She was living in one half of a duplex suite while her inlaws occupied the other. When her father-in-law was alive, every day after work he would knock on her window and wave as he walked across the lawn.

It seems that the man was determined to continue this daily ritual even after he passed on. A little after five o'clock on the day after her father-in-law's funeral, Adele's head shot up when she heard a light rapping on her front window. All she could do was gape in surprise at the sight of the deceased man as he waved at her and walked out of sight toward his duplex suite.

Adele flew out of her seat and ran next door, but her mother-in-law did not tell a miraculous story of her own to corroborate what Adele had just experienced. The man had not come back from the dead. So what had Adele just seen? She tried to convince herself that the vision was some sort of hallucination. Grieving people have often seen deceased loved ones, as their eyes and ears may be unwilling to accept the sudden absence of a person they used to see on a daily basis.

It became obvious soon enough, however, that Adele's grief and her father-in-law's apparition were not connected in any way. The man's likeness returned at the exact same time the next day. Once again, he rapped on the window, smiled, waved and then suddenly disappeared. This ghostly sequence continued daily for months on end. He appeared before no one but Adele. Her surprise soon gave away to fascination, and she became determined to learn more about the supernatural.

She enrolled herself in a parapsychology evening class. There she learned about Ghost Tours of New Hope. An organized tour through the streets of the town, the nocturnal walk took people to some of the most haunted locations in New Hope. She and Ghost Tours' founder Adi-Kent Thomas Jeffrey hit it off the moment they met.

Adi-Kent, a journalist and former model who holds a degree in parapsychology, was one of the big personalities in New Hope.

After Adele had been on her second tour, Adi-Kent asked her to become a tour guide. Adele was so good at what she did that when Adi-Kent moved to Jersey, she entrusted management of the operation to Adele, asking only that Adele not change anything in the tour. "It's been 10 years since I took Ghost Tours over," Adele says today, "and I haven't changed a thing."

Not that there's any reason to. At one time or another, Adele Gamble has had firsthand supernatural experiences at most of the stops on her tours. However, it seems that the spirit of the blond hitchhiker and the ghost of Joseph Pickett are the most inclined to put on a show for spectators.

Adele's startling first meeting with the deceased Joseph Pickett took place about 20 years ago during a Halloween séance. Ms Gamble had just begun pursuing her interest in ghosts, and she was not quite as attentive as she could have been throughout the séance. While the other paranormal enthusiasts were concentrating on bringing forth the ghost of the former artist and butcher, Adele was idly looking around the old building, somehow convinced that nothing was going to happen. She was wrong.

"It was toward the end of the séance," Adele recalls, "and I felt that something or someone lean over and grab my hair." It was a sharp tug, and, as Adele's head was yanked back, she yelled out in fear, "Adi, something has me!"

Everyone in the room spun around to see the figure of a man standing behind her. He was big, with black pants, suspenders, peppered hair and a handlebar mustache. It was Joseph Pickett, who had died more than half a century earlier. To this day, Adele believes that Pickett was put off by her distraction, and that he pulled on her hair to get her attention. "That was my introduction to Ghost Tours," Adele says today, "and I'm still there."

So is Joseph Pickett, apparently. One of New Hope's most active ghosts, Pickett has a penchant for post-mortem restlessness that is perhaps understandable, given the circumstances of his life. He was a man convinced of his own artistic genius. Unfortunately for him, none of his contemporaries seemed to appreciate his talents. Although he spent practically all his spare time painting, he was never successful enough with his art to elevate his station above that of town butcher. Not that he was at all ashamed of his profession, but the self-taught artist was hungry for some sort of recognition in the work that moved him.

The frustrated butcher went so far as to paint the entire exterior of his building in his "primitive" style so that the people of New Hope could not help but notice his art as they went about their daily business. Still, no one thought much of his work, which differed just a little bit too much from the formal paintings displayed in the art galleries of America's metropolises.

Of course, having to work in his shop by day and having no formal training in the arts did not help his ambitions. So it was that Pickett would go through life an artistic unknown. When he passed away in 1918, he went to his grave without any kind of public appreciation for his craft. Pickett's wife sold what she could for a pittance and burned the rest of his work.

A short while after the artist had passed on, however, his work suddenly became worth something. Paintings Pickett couldn't give away when he was alive shot up radically in value. His *Manchester Valley,* which now hangs in the Museum of Modern Art, is currently valued in the millions.

Has Joseph Pickett remained behind to enjoy the belated fruits of his labors? Or is he simply attached to the building where he spent most of his life? Whatever the case, his spirit is one of Ghost Tours' biggest draws.

Adele recalls one of her more memorable run-ins with Pickett while leading a tour: "I was taking a private party through the area, and stopped in front of Pickett's place to talk a little about his ghost. Well, I was about halfway through my story when two of the girls in the crowd began to gesture at me, trying to get me to turn around. So I wrapped up my presentation before I looked over my shoulder to see what had distracted them, but there was nothing there. I asked them why they were pointing at me to turn around and they told me that there was a man standing behind me. As soon as they said that, I knew what had happened."

The two girls' description of the figure behind Adele matched the description of the apparition that had appeared at the séance years back—it was Joseph Pickett. When Adele informed them that they had just seen their first ghost, the men on the tour instantly grew skeptical.

"OK guys," Adele confronted them, "who do you think that was?" They replied that she had planted the man there just to scare them, to which Adele simply replied, "Fine, then where is he now?"

It was obvious to all that there was no longer anyone standing behind Adele, and the steep drop-off behind her made it impossible for anyone to get away without making a lot of noise. "Well, I'll tell you," Adele laughs today, "right about then they all turned white in the dark."

Another popular spirit on Adele's ghost tours is the phantom hitchhiker. The hitchhiker was reportedly killed some time in the 1960s, inadvertently struck by a car while hitching at night. Repeated sightings have made him one of New Hope's most recognizable spooks. Adi-Kent had included the hitchhiker in Adele's original tour, but it would be a few years before Adele would see the ghost for herself.

"It was late in the evening, quite a few years ago," Adele begins, "and another tour guide and myself were in a car, following Adi-Kent who was driving in front of us. We were coming into town along the 202 when a lone figure suddenly appeared in our headlights."

The blond-haired man was dangerously close to the road, and Adele yelled out a warning to the guide behind the wheel. The car swerved slightly, narrowly missing the man at the side of the road. Adele got a good look at him as they passed. He had blond hair, blue eyes, a brown jacket and brown pants, with a beat-up knapsack strapped to his back. He gazed ahead blankly, completely oblivious of the car speeding by him.

For a few short moments Adele was perplexed, unable to understand how the man could be standing where he was, where the side of the road dropped off into the Delaware. It was then that she realized what she had just seen. This was the same ghostly hitchhiker about which she had told so many of the people who went on her ghost tours. When they got out of their cars in New Hope, Adele was quick to question Adi-Kent about what she had just seen. Although she hadn't seen the figure her two guides were talking about, the Ghost Tours' founder smiled knowingly, "Yes Adele," she said, "that was him."

The story of the ghost hitchhiker has been corroborated by many other people in and around New Hope. Repeatedly spotted either on Bridge Street or the 202 coming into town, the apparition has caused more than one person to jump when Adele reached the "phantom hitchhiker" segment of her tour.

"There have been people on the tour who have almost been beside themselves when I mention the hitchhiker," Adele says. "Those who have reacted usually have had some past experience with the hitchhiker, either having seen him or having heard about him at one time or another. Mostly they're sort of relieved that what they've seen or heard isn't as nuts as they might have initially thought." Relieving doubts and providing information about the supernatural—all in an evening's work for Adele Gamble.

The Hounds of Colebrook Furnace

Colebrook Furnace was fired in 1791, the second iron mill to be built in Lebanon County. It was one of the state's earliest foundries, modestly smelting ores into iron well before the Industrial Revolution turned Pennsylvania into the steel king of North America. Situated near the massive iron ore deposits of the Cornwall Ore Banks, Colebrook's early success cemented Lebanon County's tight dependence on the iron industry, a relationship between labor and capital that has continued for over two centuries.

But there is more to Colebrook Furnace than ore smelting. Under the mountain of metal, money and slag that the foundry generated over the years lies a single event of deranged cruelty so hideous that it became forever ensconced in the canon of local legend. The story is still alive today, coming back to life whenever a night fog rolls into Lebanon County.

It is on dark, mist-shrouded nights that people have reported hearing the sounds of numerous dogs running outside their homes, growling, barking and yelping in an ominous cacophony. On the same nights, restless sleepers have woken from fitful dreams of fangs, fur and moonlight, startled awake by the sound of a pack of hounds in full chase or howling wildly at an obscured moon. They are the hounds of Colebrook returning from where they rest, hunting for whatever prey got away from them one cruel October day over 200 years ago.

Although time has forgotten the name of Colebrook's first furnace master, his odious nature has been well documented by consecutive generations of storytellers. He dedicated most of his spare time to satisfying his dissolute appetites, and he earned a considerable reputation as a drunken glutton who preyed on women of easy virtue. Yet what he lacked in personality, he made up in material wealth. His position as manager of Colebrook Furnace bestowed the ruffian with tremendous wealth, making him a virtual noble among the humble people living in Lebanon County at the time.

Besides whiskey, trollops and food, the furnace master's only other love was hunting, and he claimed to have the finest pack of hounds in the county. By all accounts, his boast wasn't an empty one. In every telling of the legend, all the best adjectives are saved for the furnace master's dogs, especially for the hound named Flora, the flawless leader of the pack.

Flora was the canine embodiment of everything her master was not. The sleek white hound was alert, intelligent and loyal. Whether the furnace master was making an ass of himself at the dinner table or in the room of a brothel, Flora was always by his side, watching over her master adoringly. Neither his vulgar habits nor his licentious lifestyle mattered to the faithful animal. If he was passed out drunk under an inn table, she would lick his face until he was revived from his humiliating slumber. When he was embroiled in a barroom fight that he had more than likely caused, she was right there by his side with bared fangs and raised hackles. And when he was stumbling down unlit roads late at night, liquor-addled and unsure of the way home, Flora was there to lead him to the safety of his bed.

Yet the furnace master, who was unable to understand or appreciate any kind or generous motivation, would sometimes grow resentful of Flora's protectiveness, believing that she somehow prevented him from enjoying the kind of unbarred revelry he longed for night after night. And on evenings when he was seized by particularly virulent self-destructive urges, he would make sure that Flora would stay at home, telling his servants to lock the doors right behind him and keep a close eye on the dog throughout the night so that she would not get out and ruin his carousing.

He was in just such a mood one winter evening when a fierce blizzard raged over all of Lebanon County. Leaving Flora locked up at home, the furnace master leaned against the blistering wind and blowing snow to make his way into town, intent on enjoying another evening of debauchery. A few hours and countless flagons of ale later, he stumbled out of the local tavern. The furnace master was three sheets to the wind and alone as he stumbled through the falling snow in the general direction of his home. He was in for a long walk.

His vision in the thick blizzard was muddled by the multitude of pints he had put back. He had managed to make it to the road that led to his house, but soon after he had left the town behind him, he was completely oblivious to his surroundings. One foot fell in front of the other in a staggering snow-logged pace, and as his feet turned numb in the cold winter night, the drunken man unwittingly walked right past the gates of his home.

Soon enough, the furnace master succumbed to the combination of hypothermia and inebriation. Desiring nothing more than to rest for a little while, the furnace master fell to the ground, deliriously comfortable in a lethal bed of snow.

Flora had been on edge all night. When she wasn't pacing the house in nervous strides, she would prop herself up on a windowsill to watch the snow fall and whine anxiously. Sometime late in the evening, well after the servants had gone to sleep, the tenor of her concern changed dramatically. It was then that the entire household was awakened by the sound of Flora's manic barking. The servants shot out of bed to see what was the matter, and only the quickest among them made it down to the main sitting room in time to see Flora leap through the window and out into the storm. By the time the servants reached the shattered glass, she had disappeared into the blizzard.

The snow was deep and the wind was fierce, but Flora tore through the storm effortlessly, as if guided by an unseen beacon. By the time she reached her befuddled master, he was half-covered in snow and almost unconscious. She barked in his ear, licked his face, nipped at his fingers until crimson stains trickled onto the snow, but the comatose man did not have the wherewithal to get to his feet. So Flora pulled him up by the neck of his coat with her teeth. When the furnace master was finally up, Flora led him through the snow back to his home, never loosening her bite on the hem of his coat. Both hound and master were sapped of all strength by the time they crashed through the doorway of their home.

Whatever gratitude the furnace master may have felt toward Flora for saving his life was balanced by the irritation he felt convalescing over the next several days—the nights of which, he rationalized, he could have been drinking. And so life went on as before. Flora, always to be found close to her master's side, would receive swift kicks as often as affectionate petting. It all depended on what mood moved the furnace master at any given moment.

The only thing that seemed to change after his near-death experience was his ardor for the hunt. Throughout the next year, he drove his hounds harder than ever before, and he took extra pleasure in boasting to everyone in Colebrook that nothing was as fine as his dogs in the hunt. Somehow, the furnace master came to invest all of his self-worth in the skill of this pack.

However, the man's feelings for the poor group of animals were as capricious as they were strong. The canines were mercilessly beaten one moment and fawned over the next. Although Flora, the leader of the pack, took the brunt of the unstable man's emotions, her loyalty never faltered once. All it took was a word, and she would come bounding, tail wagging eagerly, ready to do her master's bidding.

She erred in her duties only once, on a cold October day when the trees were barely holding the last few crimson leaves on their branches. The ensuing tragedy left a mark on Lebanon County still felt today.

The dogs had been growing increasingly tired from the grueling schedule the furnace master had imposed on them. Although he was able to remove the initial signs of fatigue with vicious lashes, it was not long before not even his cruel whip was enough to motivate his animals to keep up their speed. Growing increasingly incensed at his animals' inability to keep up the hunt, his rage culminated when a fox darted right before his prized Flora and she was unable to give chase. The faithful hound was exhausted.

The furnace master, oblivious to the hounds' fatigue, did not know how to respond to this failure. He stared in disbelief as the fox's red tail disappeared into the bush. A sudden silence fell over the hunting party. Not a man, horse or dog moved. No one dared look at the furnace master. Finally, Flora turned her pleading eyes upward to where her beloved master was mounted. He was looking at her with livid eyes, every crease in his face folded into an aspect of venomous hatred.

As far as the furnace master was concerned, Flora had committed the worst crime imaginable. No slap, whip or reprimand could correct what she had just done. In one ominous motion, his eyes drifted from where she stood panting to the pillar of smoke that rose into the sky from Colebrook Furnace. Without another word, the cruel man put spurs to his horse, calling for his hunting retinue to follow. A depraved smile twisted across his face as the hunting party unwittingly followed him into the maw of absolute madness.

They were crossing the charred slag-laden stretch around Colebrook Furnace within the hour. The heat from the foundry grew more intense as the party approached. The dog handlers started to get nervous, wondering what the furnace master could possibly want from his dogs in this field of industrial waste. A heavy foreboding fell over the burnt-out clearing. The hounds slowed their pace considerably. One by one, the handlers piped up about their destination. "Where are we headed, milord?" one of the furnace master's humble employees inquired. "What animal do we hope to catch here?" asked another.

They got their answer when the party had gotten close enough to the furnace that their horses would not continue any further. Dismounting from his horse, the furnace master cast his cold eyes over his pack. A malicious plan was silently twisting through his head. Shouting over the noise of the steel mill, he gestured to the enormous caldron of molten ore before giving the unbelievable order. "Throw them in!" he roared to his dumbfounded dog handlers. "Every one of them!"

He was greeted with a long silence. The only sound was the roaring of the foundry's fires. Every man knew what he had heard, but it took a few more minutes before they could convince themselves to believe it. Yet their hesitation was short-lived, for without the good favor of the furnace master, their livelihoods in the county would be ruined.

The first man who obeyed the order let out a long sigh before he hoisted one of the hounds into his arms. The dog squirmed in his arms as they approached the heat of the caldron. Turning his head so that he wouldn't see what he was about to do, the man threw the animal into the boiling pot of metal. It was all the other handlers needed. One by one, the hapless hounds were sent to their gruesome deaths.

Before long, the magnificent pack that had been gathered about the furnace master a few minutes earlier was no more. The men stood around the furnace with their heads hung low, unable to absorb what they had done.

Then a piteous whimper pierced the dreadful silence. Crouched low at her master's feet was Flora, cowed by the ferocious madness that had consumed her entire pack. Irony of all ironies, she was hiding behind the legs of her cruel master for protection. The furnace master would soon make it known that there was none to be had there.

Roaring at his men that there was one hound left, he kicked Flora from underneath him into the circle of dog handlers. Sensing what was about to happen, the large hound turned to self-defense. She hunched low and produced a rumbling growl, warning the enclosing circle of men that they were going to have a fight on their hands if they got any closer. Although the furnace master's servants were obedient enough to carry out the man's heinous orders, they were not enthusiastic enough to risk getting hurt over it. They hesitated.

It was then that the furnace master revealed the depths of his depravity. Chiding his men as cowards, he whistled for Flora and called her name, the tone of his voice suggesting that they were going to go on a Sunday walk. She bolted into the furnace master's arms, barking and licking the man's face. The furnace master picked up the same dog that had once saved his life and carried her toward the caldron. Legend has it that the dedicated hound did not take her eyes off her beastly master during her final moments. She yelped once and then she was gone.

The furnace master turned and walked away. Without a word to any of his handlers, he mounted his horse and rode across the charred landscape that surrounded

Colebrook Furnace. He left the site of the crime alive and
well, without a single visible scar to show for the travesty
that had just taken place. But like so many injustices, evil
deeds seldom vanish into the air after they are committed.
Although the furnace master left the steel mill physically
untouched that day, the stern hand of justice planted the
seed of destruction in the twisted man's psyche. Even as
he rode home from the foundry, he knew that something
in him had changed.

Shadows came to life in the fading light of that dying
October day. Everywhere he saw animal eyes staring
out from the surrounding woods. Every sound took on
another, absolutely sinister, kind of life. Dry, leafless
branches rattling in the wind made him shiver with dread.
Cracking twigs and rustling vegetation became warnings
of inhuman predators watching him with malevolent
eyes. And he could have sworn that he repeatedly heard
a number of creatures loping behind him on padded feet.

Standing and turning in his saddle on more than one
occasion, the furnace master's fear continued to grow
until he finally set spurs to his horse and galloped for
home. The last thing he heard before he slammed the
door of his house shut behind him was the sudden sound
of countless hounds baying into the darkness. The
sound of them was so loud and so near that the furnace
master fell to the floor of his house, babbling incompre-
hensibly in mortal fear.

His servants had to pick him up from where he lay and
carry him to his bed, where he tossed and turned in
a nightmarish haze throughout the night. Things would
only get worse for the furnace master in the upcoming

days. Although he tried to drink himself into oblivion during the following night, his crass cheer was replaced by a silent anxiety that grew with every pint he drank down. He behaved so awkwardly that night that even his rough fraternity of friends didn't want anything more to do with him. And if his night at the local tavern wasn't bad enough, the lonesome ride back home terrified him so much that he was a blubbering fool by the time he returned. It would be the last time he would venture out.

The rest of his days were spent in the confines of his bedroom, thrashing madly under a heavy blanket of debilitating fear. He tried to drink his panic away, but the more he drank, the worse he got. The first night he stayed in his room, he woke the entire household with piercing, almost childish, shrieks of fear. When his servants burst into his bedchamber, they found the furnace master cowering against the wall opposite the window, hysterically pointing out at the moonlit night. The servants drew the curtains and kept a nurse there to care for him, but there would be no remedy for the mysterious mental illness that had overtaken him.

A few nights later he broke out of the restraints his servants put him in and clawed open the curtains. Hard moonlight flooded into the room, and the furnace master recoiled from the window, falling onto his bed and foaming at the mouth in some sort of incomprehensible agony. His alarmed servants looked from where he lay to the open window in front of them, but all that was visible there was a cold autumn night covered in fog and dimly lit by an obscured full moon.

The furnace master managed to get out only a few words before the trauma of the unveiled window stopped his heart. Gasping his last breath through tightly clenched teeth, he managed a last cry for help. "They're coming for me!" he screamed to his servants. "The hounds! The hounds! Flora!"

He died the moment after he yelled his favorite dog's name, and it was at that instant when howls from a pack of hounds filled the entire house. It sounded as if the dogs were right below the bedroom window. Although none of the servants openly acknowledged it at the time, everyone was certain that the baying dogs heard that night were the same animals that had been needlessly killed at Colebrook Furnace.

Over two centuries have passed since the tragedy at Colebrook. Yet, time and again, be it summer or winter, fall or spring, people have spotted a magnificent pack of hounds racing through Lebanon County at night when fog and a full moon bathe the landscape in an ethereal silver light. At the head of the pack is an enormous snow-white hound, her snout wrinkled and her fangs bared, flying after some unseen prey.

The Spirits of Hawk Mountain

For the majority of visitors to Hawk Mountain, the wooded promontory rising on the eastern side of the Appalachian range in Berks County is a world-class lookout point for bird-watchers. Every fall, thousands of ornithologists flock to Hawk Mountain Sanctuary to catch sight of the innumerable raptors making their yearly migration south. It is an amazing spectacle in which approximately 18,000 hawks, falcons and eagles of various species soar over the mountain between late August and mid-December. Nature lovers and bird-watchers alike will agree that these southbound birds of prey couldn't pick a better spot for their aerial exhibition. Hawk Mountain is one of the most beautiful spots in Pennsylvania, with a lofty summit situated high over the sprawling scenic beauty of the state's Appalachian Ridge. Those uninterested in the birds in the air need only look down to catch sight of the breathtaking vista unfolding before them.

These natural attractions bring in most of the mountain's estimated 70,000 visitors, but there is something else about the bird sanctuary that attracts a small group of people. Pennsylvania's paranormal enthusiasts know Hawk Mountain for things completely unrelated to birds or natural splendor. For deep in the bosom of the imposing mountain lie dark, sinister, secrets—tales of murder and madness that are tied to virulent and evil forces.

Charles J. Adams III, a famous Pennsylvania paranormal investigator and storyteller, has addressed the legend of Hawk Mountain in each of his three books on the ghosts of Berks County. Uncovering the dark history of the Appalachian peak, Mr. Adams explores the gruesome events that have taken place there over the course of the last three centuries, suggesting a number of different reasons for the bizarre occurrences that continue to take place today.

Hawk Mountain's ominous history began in the 18th century. In *Ghost Stories of Berks County: Book One,* Adams states that the hill was frequented by the Lenni Lanape Indians, who inhabited the area centuries before Europeans arrived. Remains of an Indian ceremonial ring found on the mountain suggest that it may have been the site for sacred rituals. When encroaching European settlers began moving across Pennsylvania in the 18th century, the local Indians were not too willing to give up the area.

The tensions that existed between white settlers and indigenous peoples are recurring themes in American history. When increasing numbers of homesteaders moved onto traditional Indian lands, violence was the all-too-frequent outcome. A small chapter in this ongoing struggle for the continent played itself out on Hawk Mountain during the winter of 1756, when a group of Indians attacked a family of homesteaders that had just set up a crude cabin on the frontier. The entire family was massacred, save one survivor—an 11-year-old boy named Jacob Gerhardt, who had managed to find a safe hiding spot in a copse of trees while his kin were put to the hatchet and his home was burned to the ground.

Exhibiting true pioneer tenacity, Jacob retained the title to his family's land on the side of Hawk Mountain. He built a stone house on the foundations of the destroyed cabin. It was there, on the original Gerhardt plot, near the

Lenni Lenape ceremonial ring and Jacob's house, that most of the hauntings have been reported.

It is not certain, however, if the strange incidents that are reported at Hawk Mountain are a result of the Gerhardt family massacre. Certainly, many believe ghosts are the residual energies that are left behind after sudden or traumatic loss of life, and the Gerhardt deaths would definitely qualify as such. But the massacre of the frontier family has not been the only evil committed on the Appalachian slope. Far from it.

Sometime in the mid-19th century, years after Jacob Gerhardt passed away, Matthias and Margaret Schambacher bought the real estate on Hawk Mountain. They transformed the Gerhardt house near the peak into a roadhouse tavern, serving those who traveled the road winding through the Appalachians. The Schambachers were new in the area, but they were the kind of people who made a strong impression, and it wasn't long before the Pennsylvanians living around the mountain had formed opinions about them. Not one of the locals had anything nice to say.

Keeping a distance from the surrounding community, the Schambachers were said to have gone so far as to ignore simple greetings. Margaret herself was scarcely, if ever, seen outside the house, and those who ran into Matthias on any given day would have wished that the same went for him. No one articulated the menace that surrounded the mysterious man, but it was there—as real as the acrid stink of his well-worn work clothes, and the hard lines that creased his face into a permanent look of hatred.

Matthias did not say a word to anyone and spent the rest of his life on Hawk Mountain without making a single friend. The only people who could claim any contact with him were the travelers passing through who ended up spending the night at his tavern. Judging by the sudden haste with which the tavern's patrons left the area after spending a night, the Schambachers were best forgotten. And those were the individuals who had the good fortune of coming out of the tavern in one piece.

Dark rumors about the couple began to spread soon after they arrived in the area. Visitors to the tavern who had paused long enough to speak to anyone after spending a night swore they would never go back up to the Schambachers. They whispered of an evening fraught with terror—of strange noises coming from the barn, of slow footsteps in the middle of the night stopping at their doors, of a very real, unsettling feeling that they were in imminent danger.

Other stories circulated as well. There were locals who ventured onto Schambacher's land and spied Matthias at work in his barn, scrubbing blood off the floor and walls. Some claimed that their horses would suddenly balk the moment they hit the outer boundaries of the Schambacher property, shying away from some intangible force that the riders could not sense. On winter nights, inexplicable flashing lights lit up the side of the mountain, while low, lingering wails drifted down form the wooded heights. No one ventured up onto Hawk Mountain at night.

All the suspicions about Matthias' murderous character were confirmed during the last months of his life, when he was struck by a fatal illness that left him bedridden and in a state of feverish delirium. It was then that he confessed to his doctor that he had killed 11 men while he lived on Hawk Mountain. The physician could only stare in silent horror as the dying murderer made his demented disclosure. "But doctor," Matthias gasped through tortured breaths, "those horrible acts, yes, they were committed by my hands, but it was not I who carried them out. There is a great evil that lives on this mountain, a devilish presence that whispers evil always, tirelessly. Murder, it has hissed into my ear late in the night when I try to sleep. Murder, at dawn's first light. Murder, when the sun is high over the hills. When I killed, it was this voice, this demonic power, that possessed me."

Then Matthias Schambacher passed away. His dying words burned an indelible mark on the folklore of Berks County, branding both his stone house and the mountain among the state's most common supernatural legends. While the reader may take such legends for what they are, subsequent events on Hawk Mountain have only added to its infamy.

Not long after Matthias passed away, another man, also by the name of Matthias, made Hawk Mountain his home. Matthias Berger, however, was completely unlike his predecessor of the same name. A kind-hearted recluse who built a rustic cabin on the side of the mountain, Matthias was a man of modest means, making what little money he had by assisting those who lived in the area with various chores. He was a devout Catholic, living every detail of his life in strict concordance with the gospels. Those who knew the beneficent hermit never ceased to be amazed by the poor man's generosity, and it wasn't long before he attained an aspect of sainthood in the eyes of his neighbors. He began holding services on the Sabbath. The surrounding community developed enough confidence in Matthias' good standing with God that they began taking their children to him for baptism in a creek that ran down the mountain. An enormous makeshift cross that he had constructed looked over his hermitage. It seemed that whatever demons had possessed Matthias Schambacher were dispelled by the good Matthias Berger.

That was until an especially dry spring in 1890. In his book *Berks the Bizarre,* Charles Adams notes the dearth of rain that fell on Berks County that spring, turning the whole of the landscape into potential kindling. Besides the fear of an inferno, Pennsylvanians living near Hawk Mountain had difficulty expressing the anxiety that suddenly hung in the air. It may have been likened to smoke from a distant fire—no one knew where the blaze was raging, but they knew it was there, hanging in the air all around them, sour and caustic.

Of course, no actual fire had erupted in the hills, but everyone knew by the feel in the air that something evil was afoot. They found out what it was before long. Late in June, a solitary hiker walking through the woods of Hawk Mountain decided to visit Matthias Berger. The sight that greeted him when he approached the hermit's home made him freeze with horror. The door to the cabin was ripped off its hinges, pieces of the primitive furniture Matthias had made lay strewn about the clearing outside the cabin, pots, pans and cutlery were scattered through the dirt, the cross that stood over his clearing had been torn down and dismantled. There was no sign of Matthias anywhere.

After a search party was organized, nearby residents combed Hawk Mountain for any sign of Matthias. Days of searching passed without a sign, until a grisly discovery was made on a rocky slope. Matthias' badly decomposed body lay twisted on the earth, ripped apart by the scavengers and reeking of death in the hot summer afternoon. Although there were a number of theories concerning Matthias' death, no suspects were ever named. Locals could not comprehend who would do such a thing, or why such an act would be committed. The crime itself went unsolved, but throughout the investigation Matthias Schambacher's final confession gained ever-increasing currency. The dark force had returned, and Hawk Mountain was once again a place of menace and shadow where few dared to venture.

And so it has remained. During the 20th century, Hawk Mountain evolved from a reclusive summit in rural Pennsylvania to the prized bird sanctuary it is today. Hermits and murderers have been replaced by wildlife personnel and eager ornithologists. Yet there is still good reason to believe the spirits on Hawk Mountain persist.

The origins of the contemporary Hawk Mountain Sanctuary go back to 1938, when a New Yorker by the name of Mrs. Raymond Ingersoll purchased the original Schambacher homestead and donated it to the newly established bird sanctuary. Some of the earliest accounts of unnatural phenomenon were reported by Hawk Mountain staff, naturalists, wildlife managers and sanctuary curators, who were living in the Schambacher house while they were employed with the sanctuary. Spine-tingling wails would suddenly pierce the silence of a dark night, as if someone in the wood was being subjected to some horrible torture. At times, the hideous cry seemed to come from a distance, drifting faintly down the mountain. On other occasions, the scream was loud and shrill—close, as if the tortured soul was merely a few yards away.

Opinion is divided on what the sound is. The more rigorous scientists who have heard it try to explain the wail as the cry of some rare nocturnal woodland animal. Detractors of this theory can't help but evoke the dark legend of the mountain they inhabit, bringing up the long history of murder and possession afflicting Hawk Mountain. These assertions arouse a considerable degree of skepticism, but other phenomena continue to keep the legends alive.

The same flashing lights that locals saw on the mountain when Matthias Schambacher made his home there over a century ago continue to be seen today. They appear on moonless nights as circular balls of light in the woods, blinking on and off erratically. Witnesses have claimed that the forest grows unnaturally quiet when these ominous lights come to life, as if every living thing on the mountain suddenly stops, enthralled by the supernatural display lighting up the darkness of the night. There is not a soul who has looked upon these lights without feeling a profound unease. It is a reaction that goes beyond the inexplicable nature of the lights; those who have set eyes on the phenomenon later said they were instantly hit with the impression that whatever was in the woods did not want them to be there. Those who have heard the wails or seen the lights would surely agree that whatever force resides on Hawk Mountain doesn't seem to be friendly.

Morbid relics from the past have only confirmed the intangible hostility on the mountain. Over the years, buried human remains have been found around the old Schambacher residence, a disturbing reminder of the horrible things that happened there. Visiting psychics drawn to the Hawk Mountain legend invariably report feeling a vague sense of hostility around Matthias Schambacher's old stone building.

While history and current experience continue to affirm the existence of some sort of supernatural menace on Hawk Mountain, what this force is exactly is another question altogether. Some paranormal enthusiasts point to the malevolent spirit of Matthias Schambacher, who still harbors an intense dislike for any living, breathing thing. Others bring up Schambacher's deathbed confession, stating that whatever forces possessed him over a century ago may still exist, continuing to express an ancient and unknown displeasure to this very day. Some theorists choose to go back even further, bringing up the specter of the original massacre on Hawk Mountain in the 18th century, when the Lenni Lenape took the hatchet to the Gerhardt family. And then there are those who emphasize the American Indians in the area, who may well have considered the mountain hallowed ground. Could it be that ancient Indian spirits, forgotten and angry, are responsible for the disturbing events that take place there?

It is quite possible that the mystery of Hawk Mountain will remain unsolved, leaving paranormal enthusiasts perennially guessing at the causes behind the hauntings.

But for the vast majority of those visiting the sanctuary, birds, not ghosts, are the main attraction, and the hill's dark history is relegated to nothing more than a footnote.

Most visits to the sanctuary pass without a single strange occurrence. Nevertheless, the legend of Hawk Mountain persists among those Pennsylvanians inclined to dwell on the paranormal, and the famous mountain rising out of the Appalachian verdure is a prime destination for nature lovers and ghost hunters alike. We can only hope that the ghosts of the formerly secluded mountain appreciate the attention, though given the record of past events and the tenor of current sightings, that does not seem probable.

Spirits in Southern Chester County

London Britain Township, nestled in the southeast corner of Pennsylvania near the small town of Landenberg, may seem an unlikely setting for a supernatural legend. Quiet, out of the way and unassuming—there is little about the township or the people who inhabit it that would suggest any tendency toward the fantastical. But, as is so often the case where the supernatural is concerned, it is not the face of the place today but the contours of its past that bind the dead to the land of the living. And there is plenty of history in London Britain.

The township was settled by Europeans in the 1700s— quite long ago by white standards in North America, but a mere blip compared to American Indian settlement in the area. Indeed, the Delaware Indians in the region have claimed that the current township stands on the site of one of their oldest towns, Minguannan Indian Town. Artifacts found there, which date as far back as 6000 BC, certainly support the assertion.

Today, the former site of the ancient Delaware settlement is marked by a boulder inlaid with a bronze plaque, a reminder of what was lost when Europeans took the region over early in the 18th century. Although long since reduced to a single thread in the tapestry of American history, Minguannan seems to retain something from the countless generations who lived and died along White Clay Creek. This feeling, at times nothing more than a sensation in the air, is especially pronounced where David Sat Rock juts out into White Clay Creek.

There really isn't much to the story of David Sat Rock. Yet it is precisely the simplicity of the ghostly account that makes it so disturbing. The legend goes back to the mid-18th century. David was an energetic young lad with a keen mind who enjoyed frequent rambles through the surrounding countryside. The rambunctious child had no way of knowing that there are some things in the wild that are as unconcerned about the fate of mortals as they are about a child's innocence—dark shadows in the woods, neither beast nor man, that cannot be explained by the rational mind.

While David was on one of his excursions, his eyes fell on a large boulder jutting out of White Clay Creek. The rock's sides were rounded by the eternal current that flowed around it. Its flat, white and clean top was somehow grooved into a perfect seat, as if centuries of layabouts had molded the boulder into a contoured sitting stone. The presence of the Delaware in the region dates back thousands of years, and many generations of American Indians may have helped to shape the rock into such an appealing seat.

Later on, David would be unable to recall what had been going through his head when he first saw the massive stone, though he remembered a powerful force that seemed to draw him toward the boulder. It was as if his legs were carrying him to White Clay Creek under their own volition. After that, David remembered nothing.

David's family had gotten used to the boy's lengthy explorations, but as the sun began to set that day, they began to worry about David. When the next morning came and he was still missing, his family feared the worst.

In actuality David was OK—or nearly OK, as it turned out. He was found the next afternoon, sitting on the boulder in the creek, staring blankly ahead, oblivious to the familial concern orbiting around him.

He was retrieved from his perch, and family members either embraced him in grateful relief or scolded him for what they perceived as inconsiderate mischief. They were about to find out that there were far more sinister forces at work on White Clay Creek than childish tomfoolery. Some of them noticed it almost instantly. The spark in the boy's eyes was missing, and his face was pale and somehow haggard, as if he had aged several years during the night he had spent on the rock. He appeared unable to answer his parents' anxious queries and could not remember anything of the last day.

His family optimistically concluded that he was either recovering from shock or simply exhausted. However, the years passed with David caught in the same sullen silence. Before the day he had spent sitting on the rock, David had been a lively boy, eager to explore everything around him, but after his mysterious experience by the creek, he sank into an inexplicable torpor, rarely venturing far from his home. For the rest of life, he was unable or unwilling to talk about what he had seen that night at White Clay Creek.

David's stilted, silent life went on for many lonely years. The community was never able to get over its suspicion of David's sudden transformation. Whispers of "the devil" and "witchcraft" followed him wherever he went, and, when he passed away, he did not have a single friend in London Britain.

Reports of a semitransparent young boy seen sitting on the rock in White Clay Creek began to spread soon after David was buried. More than one man came back from hunting, wide-eyed and mumbling fearfully about the apparition. It was a young boy staring blankly into the waters flowing around him, they said. When they approached him, they would be startled to find that they could see right through his image, discerning the glint of sun on the water behind him as well as the rustling foliage flanking the creek. In another moment, the apparition would simply vanish into thin air, leaving the startled witness baffled.

People quickly connected the phenomenon with David. Not long afterward, locals began referring to the boulder as David Sat Rock, after the unfortunate boy whose life was forever changed after his unknown experience on that same stone.

To this day, people still see the boy's apparition perched on the boulder in 18th-century dress, staring intently at some mysterious vision in the flowing waters of White Clay Creek. Is he staring at some ineffable chronicle of the people who inhabited the land in the millennia before he lived there? Perhaps he is still paying the price for sitting on a stone that was once sacred. From the perspective of the living, of course, one explanation is as good as the next, and we can only hope that young David will one day abandon his solitary vigil in White Clay Creek to rest in a long-deserved peace.

It is safe to say that most of the people who turn off the SH1 and navigate Pennsylvania's side-roads with the intention of taking a look at the David Sat Rock are supernatural devotees. However, there is more than one paranormal wonder in the southern reaches of Chester County. An unusual feeling is nowhere more obvious than at London Tract Baptist Church. In the small cemetery behind this humble house of worship stands the famous Ticking Tombstone. Such is the reputation of this particular grave marker that paranormal buffs from all over the nation have stopped by this out-of-the-way hamlet to see—and hear—for themselves what transpires in the secluded cemetery.

At first glance, nothing about the Ticking Tombstone would strike anyone as especially strange. It is simply a slab of unadorned rock lying flat, level with the surrounding ground and carved simply with two initials, "R.C." Anyone expecting a gravestone of gothic splendor is sure to be disappointed. But the marvel of the object is auditory, not visual.

To appreciate the Ticking Tombstone, a visitor must get close to the stone's surface. The sound is so faint that witnesses have heard it only when their ears have been pressed flat against the grave. One almost has to concentrate to hear it, but once it is identified among all the casual noises on the earth's disquieted surface, it becomes impossible to ignore. From somewhere under the tombstone it emanates, as constant today as it was a hundred years ago—a barely audible, perfectly measured ticking.

A number of theories attempt to explain the origins of the Ticking Tombstone, and some of them seem as far-fetched as any other supernatural story circulating in the state. One legend has a baby boy swallowing a timepiece belonging to Charles Mason, one of the head surveyors of the Mason–Dixon Line between the slave states and free states prior to the Civil War. The child grew to adulthood, the story continues, with the watch in his stomach. Somehow, the timepiece was able to survive the acidic conditions in the man's stomach and continued to function throughout the man's life. And, supposedly, the watch functions still, making the ticking heard faintly under the tombstone of the mysterious R.C.

But this story hardly explains why the ticking seems to grow louder during the rainy months. Skeptics have theorized that the sound emanating from the tombstone isn't really ticking but dripping. This story maintains that a small underground cavern lies not too far underneath the tombstone, and the repetitive noise is actually ground-water dripping into the this hidden reservoir. The sound increases after a heavy rainfall, the theory goes, when the precipitation seeps through the ground and splashes into the collecting pool of water below. Not a very spectacular story, but one that would probably be regarded as the most rational explanation for the sound emanating from the Ticking Tombstone.

The most popular account about the tombstone, however, happens to be the most improbable one. Once again, we return to the creation of the Mason–Dixon Line. In this version, the timepiece does not belong to Charles Mason but to a man in his surveying crew whose name history has forgotten. The crew was busy mapping out the Circle (the name given to the semi-circular border arcing between upper Delaware and Pennsylvania), when the hapless surveyor was brutally murdered.

A gloomy day was ending with heavy rain when the man's fellow workers discovered his body beside a river. The mutilated corpse lay twisted on the bank, completely oblivious to the streams of freezing water rushing over his legs, streaming down his motionless arms and pooling in the twin basins of his open eyes.

He had been killed by an unknown perpetrator for unknown reasons. The homicide was destined to go down as one of the region's unsolved mysteries, and la minor one at that. But future generations would connect the strange ticking coming from the flat tombstone with the memory of the horribly murdered survey man, and he would be resurrected for the tale of the Ticking Tombstone.

The story goes that the only possession the murdered man carried was a chronometer, still ticking, buried in his pants pocket. Out of respect, the surveying crew left it on his person, and he was buried with instrument laid on his chest. His co-workers carved his initials into his modest tombstone and carried on with their work, leaving the man to rest forever in the quiet cemetery of the London Tract chapel.

As is the case with many others who have met a violent end, however, the survey man's rest was not a peaceful one. Ever since he was buried there, passers-by could hear the sound of faint ticking underneath his tombstone, it is said. At first, residents stated that the sound likely came from the chronometer that was buried with the man. But, as years turned to decades, and even after the body was certainly relegated to dust, visitors to the cemetery could still hear the instrument ticking away. No one believed that any kind of machinery could be built so well as to last this long, still functioning long after the subterranean forces of entropy would have claimed almost anything else.

The Ticking Tombstone was soon given supernatural attributes. The locals reminded each other of the Mason–Dixon survey worker and the unsolved murder. Perhaps the sound of the ticking timepiece signified a supernatural resolve, the immortal patience of the dead man's spirit as he waits for a vindication that will never come. That the ticking gets more audible when it rains, sounding an ominous beat through the entire cemetery, only cements the theory of the dead man's spirit further. "Was he not killed on a rainy day?" people ask. Wouldn't the sound, smell and feel of rain falling remind the spirit of the terrible day he lost his life, and make his ghost angrier? Many people believe so.

Regardless of which explanation ones chooses to believe, there is no mistaking the ticking sound faintly emanating from the inconspicuous tombstone that lies behind the London Tract Baptist Church. Unrelenting and somehow ominous, the tombstone appears to be waiting for an unforeseen calamity that has not yet come to pass. What is the impending disaster? Perhaps only the silent souls buried under the surface know for sure.

The Song of Sweet Cicely

This story takes us back to the mid-1800s, before Andrew Carnegie created a corporate empire from Pittsburgh steel and when the Mauch Chuck Switchback (the forerunner to the roller coaster) was considered a technological innovation. Yet, even as the big ball of North American civilization was just beginning its roll, there were already a number of American Indian cultures that were being squashed under it.

The trials of tribes such as the Wampanoag, Narragansett and Iroquois would be the writing on the wall for subsequent Indian groups that had yet to come into contact with the colonizers from the east. Even for those Native Americans who were able to survive the diseases brought by the Europeans and adapt to their foreign ideas of order, the temper of early American society made them irreconcilable outsiders in their own land.

Years had passed since the Mingo Indians had been driven west from their traditional grounds in the woods of Ohio and Pennsylvania to the arid plains of Oklahoma.

Although Powderhorn was conscious of the changes afoot, he was one of the few Mingo who stubbornly remained behind, unwilling to leave the land of his people.

Powderhorn and his wife resided in current-day Sylvan Dell, near Williamsport. Among their eight daughters and one son, a single girl stood out as the jewel of the family. Everyone knew there was something special about her from the day she was born. She was named Sweet Cicely after the sweet and delicate healing plant that flourished throughout the region.

Sweet Cicely was a sensitive, serene and intelligent child who became the kind of beautiful woman that legends are made of. Unfortunately, stories of women with such spectacular grace seldom end well, and like Helen of Troy or Anna Karenina, the Indian maiden would suffer for her charms. Before she became the tragic beauty of the Loyalsock, however, she was just a simple young woman in love with a simple young man.

A local Mingo youth named Wild William had known Cicely since he was a boy. As they matured, the couple developed a deep attachment for one another. By the time they reached adulthood, the two were practically inseparable. If William was not laboring on Ezra McGrady's farm across the river from Powderhorn's home, he was sure to be found in Sweet Cicely's company. They spent most of their hours together sitting on a stone ledge that hung about 10 feet above the racing Loyalsock, talking about their future hopes as the water rushed by beneath them. Cicely would wait there for her beau at the end of every working day, singing happily to herself as she tossed pebbles into the creek. Her voice was clear as the waters before her, and carried for miles downstream. Before long, she was famous among the raftsmen who navigated the Loyalsock in springtime. The hardened men that made their living there spoke gently when their conversation turned to the singing woman. "A voice like an angel," they muttered in wonder about Sweet Cicely, "and beautiful like no one else."

Their reverence for the girl transcended any racist assumptions about the American Indians in the area, and every man along the Loyalsock was smitten with starstruck admiration for the woman on the rock ledge. Whenever these men caught site of Sweet Cicely and Wild William perched upon their lookout point over the stream, they waved enthusiastically and shouted greetings at the couple.

These salutations were always returned with kindness. It even seemed for a short time that Lycoming County might become the one exception to the violent patterns that defined Indian–American relations throughout the rest of the United States. But, alas, in every Eden there must be a serpent, and the idyllic happiness that thrived along the Loyalsock was cruelly brought to an end by one covetous murderer.

Legend does not remember the name of the man who stared at Sweet Cicely with lustful hatred late one spring night, but his iniquitous deed on that awful evening killed the hopeful spirit of the young community along the Loyalsock.

The story goes that Wild William was late in joining his lover on their rock one night, and Cicely was passing the time as she usually did. She was singing an old Indian ballad that began with the words, "Wild roved an Indian girl, bright Alfarata." It is said that the tune was so bewitching that the entire forest grew silent in order to hear some of Cicely's song. The sun sank lower and the shadows in the woods deepened as every sylvan creature around the stream listened curiously to the vocal strains rising above the sound of the water.

The song also caught the attention of one raftsman who was looking for a place to pull up and rest for the night. Like everyone else who navigated the riffles of the Loyalsock, the man knew of Sweet Cicely and Wild William. But this man had no fond feelings for the Mingo couple. In fact, there was something about their happiness that stirred a profound hatred in his heart, and, when he heard Cicely's song that evening, his mind was possessed by evil thoughts.

He beached his raft under the rock ledge and made his way up to where Sweet Cicely was sitting. None of the rafters had ever tried to approach her before. Surprised at this man's advance, Cicely, puzzled, stopped singing and looked on, not sure of what to do. Minutes later, when the man stood on the ledge before her with an all-too-evident hatred burning in his eyes, it was too late for her to run.

Their struggle was brief. When the raftsman could not get what he wanted from her, he wrapped his hands around her throat and crushed her windpipe. She died on that same ledge where she had spent the happiest moments of her life.

Wild William had just finished his duties at Ezra McGrady's farm when he caught sight of the murderer clambering up the cliff toward his love. Rowing frantically across the river toward her, he witnessed the assault on Sweet Cicely firsthand. The deed was done by the time he reached their lookout point. Sweet Cicely was dead, and her assailant had escaped through the dense wood in a panic, leaving his boat behind on the bank. Denied his love and even his right of vengeance, William collapsed on the cliff top, overcome with grief.

Things were never the same in Sylvan Dell after that. The Powderhorn family tried to compensate for their loss through legal channels, but at the time American laws did little to protect Indians. They left Pennsylvania soon afterward to join extended family in the Indian Territory. Wild William wandered off as well, carrying a heavy load of grief for the rest of his days.

Sweet Cicely, on the other hand, did not appear so eager to leave Sylvan Dell. Ezra McGrady's farm was across the stream from where the Powderhorn family had lived, and McGrady could see Sweet Cicely's ledge from his farmhouse. During the first few years after the murder, the strains of beautiful music would sometimes drift through his home late in the afternoon.

It was always in the spring, always the same song, the one that begins with "Wild roved an Indian girl, bright Alfarata"—the tune that Cicely sang the night she was murdered. The first few times he heard the song, the farmer went running out to the Loyalsock to see who might be there, an impossible hope pounding in his chest. Although the woman's voice, strong and clear, grew louder as he neared Cicely's cliff, there was never anyone there.

In the years following Cicely's murder, there was a dramatic increase in the number of deaths on Loyalsock

Creek. Although the rocky stream was never an easy one to navigate, experienced raftsmen were usually careful enough to make it through without too much trouble. But now there were stories of a young woman's voice rising over the waters, singing a song of such beauty that the hapless pilots on the Loyalsock were instantly struck dumb by the sound of the unseen woman's voice. It was then, when they were mesmerized by the phantom chanteuse, that some rock on the Loyalsock would claim their vessel. A few moments of distraction was all it would take to send these men, their rafts and their cargo into the swift-flowing creek. For a short while, the stretch of the Loyalsock near Ezra McGrady's farm became infamous for these wrecks.

McGrady's home turned into a regular stop for the raftsmen on the creek. Those who managed to keep their vessels afloat when the mysterious voice sang usually pulled up at McGrady's farm with a number of awe-inspired questions. In the discussions that followed, Sweet Cicely's name was mentioned in fearful, wonderstruck whispers.

Years passed, and every spring the locals expected Sweet Cicely's song with the same kind of certainty they lent to melting snow and budding leaves. It was during one spring a few years after the murder that McGrady was visited by a man whose attitude about the voice on the rock ledge was markedly different from that of any other raftsman who had visited before. The man was angry and drunk, and he had a scared, haggard look about him, as if he were haunted by something that was bigger than he was.

He approached McGrady with a kind of furious desperation, demanding to know what had become of the

Indian family that had lived across the river. The stranger, of course, was referring to Powderhorn's family, and Ezra immediately grew suspicious. Why was this man inquiring about Powderhorn? Did it have anything to do with Sweet Cicely, who, just a few hours previously, he had heard singing just as clearly as she had when she was alive?

After lengthy conversation, in which Ezra plied the riverman with a few more drinks, the old farmer learned what was eating away at the strung-out stranger. He was the one. It was he who had killed Sweet Cicely on that spring evening a few years ago, and he was convinced that the girl's family was responsible for the song on the Loyalsock—a deliberate attempt to drive him mad.

Feigning indifference to the man and his plight, Ezra sent him on his way after their talk, telling the killer that he was tired and wanted to sleep. But McGrady loved Sweet Cicely as much as anyone else who lived in the area, and he was determined to see justice done. "Fate sent that man here," the farmer muttered to himself as he settled down to bed, "and Indian or not, that girl will be avenged."

McGrady told the next group of raftsmen who stopped at his place all about Cicely's murderer—his name, what he looked like, the desperation in his voice. The assembled raftsmen swore they would vindicate Sweet Cicely and parted company the next day resolved to mete out justice to the vile criminal who had deprived them of their joy.

The murderer would be the next man to die on Loyalsock Creek. Legend has it that one of the raftsmen spotted the killer early the next spring. He was sighted piloting his way down the swollen stream late in the day. The sun was low, and the surrounding trees were dark.

As the criminal approached Cicely's rock, he glanced up uneasily at the looming ledge. But he need not have been afraid of Sweet Cicely that night; a much more corporeal threat was fast approaching from upstream.

A vengeful raftsman bore down on him, crashing the bow of his vessel into the unsuspecting villain's raft. The murderer was pitched overboard into the water, whereupon the swift current threw his body into every boulder in the riffles. By the time his body was washed up on the banks, he was dead, his body mangled beyond recognition.

The men on the Loyalsock buried the killer's body near Powderhorn's deserted cabin the next morning. And as they unceremoniously covered up the pit they had dug, the sudden sound of Sweet Cicely's clarion voice interrupted their labor. Her words, from the final verse of her favorite song, were as clear as the early morning sky. "Fleeting years have borne away the voice of Alfarata," she sang.

The rough men gathered by the grave were awed into silence. Hearing the words on the other side of the stream, Ezra McGrady was moved to tears at the sound of the Mingo girl's voice. Returning again for the first time that spring, she had never sounded so close or so clear.

That was the last time Sweet Cicely was heard on the Loyalsock.

The End

GHOST HOUSE

GHOST HOUSE BOOKS

The colorful history of the United States includes many spine-tingling tales of the supernatural. Fun, fascinating collections by GHOST HOUSE BOOKS reveal the diversity of paranormal phenomena nationwide. Our ghostly tales involve well-known theaters, buildings and other landmarks, many of which still bear testament to their haunted histories.

Ghost Stories of America *by Dan Asfar and Edrick Thay*
A fascinating collection of frightening stories, culled from all 50 states and reflecting more than 200 years of haunted history. Visit famous haunts such as the Alamo, the Biltmore Hotel and Fort Laramie or learn about a ghost who may live in your neighborhood.
$10.95   ISBN 978-1-894877-11-4   5.25" x 8.25"   248 pages

Ghost Stories of Michigan *by Dan Asfar*
This spirited collection features ghosts from the Great Lakes State, such as the Red Dwarf of Detroit, who turns up whenever tragedy visits, and the ghostly lighthouse keeper of White River, who continues to ply his earthly trade in a haunted hereafter.
$10.95   ISBN 978-1-894877-05-3 5.25" x 8.25"   224 pages

Ghost Stories of Indiana *by Edrick Thay*
Paranormal folklore from the Hoosier State includes the story of the football star and original "Gipper," George Gipp, who is said to roam the halls of the University of Notre Dame. Other stories involve a restless spirit still searching for his little girl at Spook Light Hill near Terre Haute and the haunting of Purdue University by the spirit of renowned aviatrix Amelia Earhart.
$10.95   ISBN 978-1-894877-06-0   5.25" x 8.25"   200 pages

Ghost Stories of Ohio *by Edrick Thay*
Ohio's rich history has given rise to a wealth of fascinating supernatural lore. From the story of a medieval dreamer who haunts the castle that was his life's passion to bizarre reports of a mysterious mothman, Edrick Thay recounts the state's most intriguing tales of the unexplained, including several eye-opening accounts of paranormal investigations at infamous haunted buildings.
$10.95   ISBN 978-1-894877-09-1   5.25" x 8.25"   192 pages

These and many more *Ghost Stories* books are available from your local bookseller or by ordering direct at 1-800-518-3541.